The Lion's Binding Oath and Other Stories

BY AHMED ISMAIL YUSUF

Catalyst Press
Livermore, California

The Lion's Binding Oath and Other Stories

For further information, write Catalyst Press,
2941 Kelly Street, Livermore CA 94551
or email info@catalystpress.org.

An early version of "A Delicate Hope" was first published
in *Bildhaan*, V 3, 2003: an International Journal of Somali Studies;
Macalester College, Saint Paul, Minnesota.

An early version of "A Thorn in the Sole" was first published
in *Bildhaan*, V 5, 2005: an International Journal of Somali Studies;
Macalester College, Saint Paul, Minnesota

"Don't Lose" originally published
in Mizna: Prose, Poetry, & Art Exploring Arab-America, 8.1 (2006).

ISBN 978-1-946395-07-8 (PBK) 978-1-946395-08-5 (EBOOK)
Library of Congress Control Number: 2018930032
Cover design by Karen Vermeulen, Cape Town, South Africa

AUTHOR'S NOTE

Raised as a nomad in Somalia, at the age of nine or eight (no one knows the exact year I was born) I surprised my mother at eight o'clock one morning, when I stood right in front of her and told her that I was tired of herding sheep and goats.

Fast forward to several years later in Harlem, New York: a relative of mine dumped two dozen books on my lap and said, "Here, you seem to have a lot of free time in your hands. Why don't you do some reading?" I was a high school dropout, my country was sitting on a hissing volcano that later exploded in the form of a civil war, and I was the only one in my family who escaped the nomadic life to the U.S.A. But I was hopelessly lost!

Embarrassed that I had never read a whole book even in Somali, I collected the books, "a challenge," from my relative's hands, realizing that I couldn't say aloud, "I have never read a book in my life!" Among the books was *I Know Why the Caged Bird Sings* by Maya Angelou, which I picked for no particular purpose whatsoever. It took me two weeks to finish it but I must have absorbed it all, for I know that book changed my life and I am forever grateful!

This book later led me to the door steps of Trinity College, in Hartford, Connecticut, where an academic advisor with a mission to teach and the will to match forced me to take an English class (my worst nightmare now) with a professor who, despite the maze of confusion in me, guided me and infused me with the love of writing.

I forever owe a debt of gratitude to these three then: my relative, Abdikadir J. Dualeh, PhD; my academic advisor and professor, Diane Zannoni; Denise Best; Louis Fisher; and my professor, my late friend Fred Pfeil.

Sincerely,

Ahmed I. Yusuf

TABLE OF CONTENTS

A Slow Moving Night

On the high mountainous land of the Sanaag region in Somalia, *jiilaal* season showed neither compassion nor mercy on its inhabitants. The trees stood still, the boughs refused to sway, even slightly, and the reflection of the sun's rays shone on rocks with flat surfaces.

A herd of sheep and goats moved about in mad fury trying to seek sanctuary under the shade of a tree, which had shrunk within the past two hours or so from a sizable length able to provide shelter to a negligible hue. Once they got under the tree and into the shade, the sheep huddled in concert. Some sat, some remained standing, and some hid their heads under the others. But the goats butted one another, competing for better positions. The day progressed slowly beyond the zenith, yet the heat persisted, driving the herd to a delirious lust for water.

One ewe finally had enough. Suddenly she broke out of the herd's temporary huddle and moved on, westward. One by one, the rest of her family flocked behind. The goats, too, left the shade but, instead of trailing the sheep, chose to scatter about, scrub grazing.

Thousands of years of experience, passed down from generation to generation, had taught herdsmen to recognize the behaviors of certain animals. Thus it was quite apparent to both my brother and me that the sheep were in search of water. It was my job and his, however, to keep them away from drinking, regardless. The reasons were many, but chief among them was that, in the dry *jiilaal* season as well as the *xagaa*, nomads in Somalia water-fed their livestock in a managed manner. We are able to weigh the severity of drought by estimating how much moisture the trees have stored in their roots and how much juice is left in their leaves. The data we gather help us decide how long a flock of sheep or goats can lust for water but continue to survive without it. It's a matter of economic grazing, calculated by the amount of available food. Trying to control the amount of water our animals are taking in, we make sure that there is enough space left in their stomachs for fodder as well.

Naturally, sheep are a bit slower and less adventurous than goats. Feeling safer in packs, they neither spread over nor ascend to the highest peaks of mountains. Goats, on the other hand, climb high on the roughest rocks, graze precariously on tilted slopes and cliff edges. Yet always alert, they rarely let a foe catch them off guard. If they ever stumble into a mishap and awaken a beast stealing a nap, they let out a high-pitched distress bleat. The sheep, however, may feast on foliage even while a coyote is goring them. And just in case you might ask, sheep baa mainly on two occasions: one, when they are looking for their broods and two, when they are in search of water. Yet both goats and sheep share a single misfortune: the need for a vigilant, tireless watcher, necessitated by a plethora of predators (hyenas, leopards, jackals, coyotes, lions, cheetahs, and men).

For his size and age, it was not an accident that my brother instinctively saw fit to follow the breakaway herd of sheep, for he knew that I, the older of the two of us and thus the stronger, was going to make him do so anyway. I would try my best to avoid sweating more than he.

From far off, the howling of baboons echoed through the

valley-beds. And to the west, a falcon soared so high in the heavens, I wondered whether it was searching for a long lost companion or was just cheerfully flying for the joy of it.

My train of thought was rudely interrupted by an army of ants approaching only inches away. I faced them as though they were an invading enemy and sized them up. I was rather disarmed by their ingenuity to serve the full circle of life. Some carried cut-away green leaves 10 times heavier than their own weight; others carried burdens weighing as much as themselves; yet some simply followed the rest in droves. I tried to trace back to their origin but saw only a tiny, dark line, snaking through the terrain.

As I followed the trail, I saw a chameleon lashing a vindictive tongue, tossing ants into his mouth and gobbling them down. He barely acknowledged me before scurrying off. I rushed forward to survey the damage he had inflicted on the delicate, almost invisible path.

The line was battered in several places. So a lonely ant, trying to go about her daily chores, appeared confused, stopped, ran, stopped and ran again. Another befuddled one ran back and forth, then left and right. Yet another, carrying a cut-away clump of leaves, veered off to the left, following an invisible map. Then a lonely one emerged from the dust and continued imperviously, as though determined to lead them all away. Alas, not a single ant followed. They no longer marched with carefree pride, and seemed to have lost that sense of marveling at the natural beauty around them.

Of course, I thought a human being should mend the mess, so I lay tiny twigs where I thought the line was broken on one end all the way to the other end where I thought that it had begun. Then I picked a twig and placed it in front of the disoriented ants. When an ant got on it, I transfered it to the line I had created with twigs. But each one declined to follow the line.

"Let them doom themselves to their stupid death," I consoled myself. "God helps those who help themselves."

Not more than a minute had passed when, to my dismay, two ants emerged from each end of the line, met in the middle, kiss-greeted, and then proceeded on their respective ways. In another minute, columns miraculously converged from opposing ends of an invisible line. A parade began on a single thread, with all now facing the same direction, as though nothing had disturbed the path.

I was about to leave when I saw another group from the same colony drag a small dead gecko with a precision that human soldiers would have difficulty matching. The unfortunate creature was turned over, her white belly blue where multiple ant bites had injected poison into her blood stream.

The army, many under the tiny gecko, latched on to the legs, transporting an eliminated foe.

The ants' ingenious, collaborative effort engaged my curiosity until suddenly the distinctive bleat of a distraught goat caught me off guard. And then it hit me that I had committed the cardinal sin that all herdsmen must avoid: you should never let your herd out of your sight. As I dashed off in the direction of the goat's plea, I heard my brother cry out from the middle of the valley-bed. I knew immediately that he had fallen off the edge of a steep slope somewhere. Ignoring the cries of the bleating goat, I took off to find him.

Frantically I ran down the slope, dislodging shells, stones, sticks and all. The cacophony of the tiny avalanche echoed throughout the valley below, causing the goats to stampede and climb the highest tip of the other side of the ridge. Heading down in a haze of confusion, I came upon Shammad, my favorite goat, who had just delivered twin kids. I could see from a distance that one of the kids was waddling, the placenta still swathed to him. I predicted a problem: that this could attract the most heinous, hideous creature of all, the spotted hyena. But I had no time to attend to them. The fear that I was going to find my brother with lacerations and broken bones besieged me. "God, please don't let it be the spinal cord," I pleaded over and over again.

My legs were about to give out. And now as I charged through the thorny underbrush, my shabby clothes were torn to pieces. But I kept on pleading with God to give my brother a chance and not penalize him for my witless neglect. I solemnly swore that if he would heed my plea today, I would never, ever again be consumed with admiration and awe of those small creatures that had rendered me mindless.

I was, as well, leery of how I was going to convince my mother later on that whatever calamity had befallen our goats happened because of "God's will." She was a severe disciplinarian and, worse, had already admonished me on numerous occasions to be vigilant to avoid all possible mishaps. I knew she was going to wail at me and bemoan my carelessness.

I began to pray for a mild beating, or better yet, a harsh scolding.

All of these thoughts collided in my head as I hurled down the steep slope. Fears for my own survival were interrupted by the cries from the sheep and my brother's piercing howls.

And then I spotted him! It looked like he was just sitting on the ground but as I came closer, I saw that he had a sheep by the leg and was pulling it away from something. When I was a few feet away, I realized that he was in a contentious tug of war with one of the most dangerous predators, the leopard. The elusive beast had strangled a thoroughbred ram and torn a slab of fresh flesh from its jowl. Blood was trickling from the wound to the ground. The leopard, crouching, looked ready to pounce. Every time my brother tried to pull the ram away, the leopard, claws fully extended, feinted to lunge but hung on with his powerful jaws. Whenever the leopard made his deceptive move, my brother would let go of the leg, jump back, and wail louder. Startled, the leopard would recoil, growling, and my brother would summon the courage to grab the leg again.

My heart froze with fear as my brother looked back at me. Not knowing how I could save him, I ducked down. My petulant brother, however, was putting up a valiant fight and expected to be bailed out or, at least, assisted.

It should not surprise you that I wanted to do just that, but could not wrench the tiniest bit of courage from my soul. Supporting my weight with one hand, I freed the other for defense and raised my head up from behind a bush. There was the leopard in full view. His sheer bulk forced me to wish that my brother would not play this game. I wondered what he was trying to prove and how on earth he was going to get out of this stalemate.

Eyes bulging, my brother looked into the brush, as though that would hasten help. The leopard rose slightly, seized the ram with his claws, and tried to snatch it away. I quickly ducked down again, praying that the leopard had not spotted me.

By now the silent ram had had enough of the pain. He baaed so loud that the rest of his family, huddled only a few feet away, felt compelled to join his plea. Contributing to the chorus of terror, my brother shrieked like a seiged soul. I yearned for the land to give way under me and begged God to deposit me back into my mother's warm womb.

"Doogle, where are you?" my brother called.

Let me tell you, I was not impressed at all that Taahe had thrown my name into the ethereal air when all he had to do was let go of the ram. We had plenty of sheep, and losing one, even a thoroughbred ram, wasn't going to make us poorer.

But Taahe continued to call me: "Doogle, show me your bravery, show me the valor you mustered when you fought off that jackal long ago!"

What my brother could not remember, because I had never told a soul, was how terrified I had been facing the jackal he was referring to.

With the misfortune of hearing my name disseminated so generously into the air, I decided to come out to defend it. Yet it dawned on me that my brother was not fair, for he was inveigling me to face the "dean of danger." This was not a jackal, and he knew it.

He would not let up. He kept the heat on, furiously fanning it. "Brother Doogle," he yelled. "The whole neighborhood knows you are brave. I know you are brave and the leopard knows you are brave. That's why I've been waiting for you, so that when he feels your aura of gallantry approaching, he will unlock his jaws, rein in his claws, and slouch away!"

I was ashen with fear and anger. Surely, the predator was going to take up his offer to challenge me at any moment now. Yet I wanted my brother to believe in me and I wanted him to keep calling me brave. And if you ask me, yes, I enjoyed it while it lasted. What I was objecting to, nevertheless, was calling me brave only if I confronted the leopard! Why could one still not be called brave if he chose a non-confrontational approach?

I was not going to show my face, because I knew that this majestic creature would cast his spell on me and I would cave in, probably whimpering with fear. I also knew that my family would scold me, that if I let the leopard have this ram for a meal he would come back for another and another and another…

I did not want to let my brother believe that I was not worthy of his praise, but still I could not move a muscle when, again, he called, "Brother Doogle, this fool leopard has not yet gotten a whiff of you. Please hurry, just come closer and he will vanish in fear from your mere presence." My brother always spoke with the maturity of unmatched eloquence.

I, on the other hand, the one who was devoid of wisdom, thought, *No, little man, no. This is a leopard, the most resourceful, elusive cat of all. Once I come out of hiding, he will cast his spell on me and leave the ram, to feast on me.*

I forced myself to crouch on all fours, as though I were about to take off at full speed. But my legs were wobbling, my hands were weak, my heart was pounding like a bouncing ball. I grabbed my spineless soul and attempted to stand upright. I was not fully erect when I began to backpedal, hoping to hide myself in the shadowed field for a moment, before galloping away at full speed.

Alas, my brother turned around and caught me in my compromising crouch. In that instant, he changed. He stopped chanting my praises and began to chide. "You coward," he barked. "Where the hell are you trying to run off to?"

Furious, I stood up, and, chin up, tossed up some phony courage. My brother was holding the ram by the leg while the leopard still clutched onto the shoulders, but once he began to shout at me, he loosened his grip. The leopard seized the moment to snatch the "meal" away.

Completely letting go of the leg, my brother dashed over and pasted himself onto me so tight that I thought a spirit had possessed him. I let him cling to me, thankful that he had let the ominous enemy loose.

In relief, my body let go. Sadly, I wet my pants just when my brother harnessed himself onto me, right after the leopard plunged his fangs into the ram's throat.

The poor ram had been instantly overpowered and was not

able to manage even a minor, convulsing move. He shivered a few, feeble twitches. It was all over.

In earnest, the killer began to tend his prey, letting go of the throat, licking the blood oozing out of gaping gashes where his fangs had penetrated, growling at us every now and then. He straddled the carcass, grasped its neck in his jaws, lifted it up, and sidle-dragged the body away—all the while, keeping an eye on us. Growling and dragging the body, he lumbered up the steep slope, behind the thick brush, beside the huge rock that seemed as if it would roll away if touched, past the dry weeds, and onto the top of the slope—where he disappeared.

Taahe released me from his clutch and let out a sigh. He took a few steps away, and started to examine me. He stopped short as he became aware of his own strange discomfort.

"Doogle," he started, looking at his pants, first one leg, then the other, then at his palms, then twisting his pants from front to back. "What...?"

"What's the matter, Taahe?" I interrupted, feeling timid.

"Do you notice that I am wet?" he asked. And to my dismay he began to get closer, examining me with a look of disgust and surprise.

"What are you talking about?" I cried, mimicking his conspiratorial gaze.

"Why am I wet?" he asked.

I wanted to come up with an ingenious way to protest my innocence by denying that I had wet my pants when fear had penetrated my total being and I could no longer will my internal organs to obey me.

"I had my period," I said, off-handed.

My brother jumped five feet away, laughing hysterically.

"Since when did men begin to menstruate?" he barked.

"Since Adam and Eve," I persisted. "Besides, what the hell do you know about men's menstruation? You are too young to know and too inexperienced to care."

"Unlike you, at least I have been around long enough to know that our Dad has never menstruated." My brother jabbed me.

"How on earth do you know that? And let me hear you clearly, are you accusing me of cowardice when I just saved your ass?"

My brother was not ready for confrontation, I guess, or perhaps he realized how desperate I had become to defend my deflated ego.

"I am only saying that I have never heard Dad or Mom or anyone else talk about this, Doogle," he said.

"I'll have you know," I said, "that women have theirs and men have theirs too. But the man type of menstruation is different from women's."

I thought I had convinced him when my brother went on to ask, "And Doogle, where does this type come out?"

Damn it, I thought. What the hell, I was going to say that men fart theirs when they are scared, but at that moment a throng of sheep that had been huddling under the trees, hugging the waterhole, suddenly stampeded toward us. I jumped up and took off, saved from any further discussion on a topic that had gotten way out of hand. My brother was not far behind.

We soon collected the rest of the herd, goaded them out of the waterhole, and moved them up the steep climb to the top of the mountain. Taahe had not exchanged a word with me on our way up. On top of the ridge where we would be able to see any enemy approaching but surrounded by steep cliffs, populated by precariously perched boulders and atrophied trees that were lean and gnarled, we let the herd graze.

Abruptly, again, we heard Shamad bleating. My favorite goat with the twin kids that I had stumbled upon earlier and then temporarily forgotten was still in danger.

I pelted away in horror, sprinting to reach her. Because of my knowledge of how jackals exercised their primal cruelty on many a goat, I thought I might be able to save her. Racing to reach my destination, it hit me that the rest of the herd of goats was nowhere in sight. Regret rose in a wave of nausea. Shamad was not just a goat. She was my treasure. She was blessed with a wealth of milk, was very friendly, and whenever I called her in the middle of the night from the corral, she would rush to reach me, while the remaining rascal goats would wait for me to sludge through their manure to get to them.

I raced from the top of the ridge, down the twisting slope to the riverbed, and up the opposite slope. With aching muscles and panting breath, I pushed forward. I could hear the rest of the goat herd in the distance, but, ignoring them, I used my remaining strength to get to Shamad. There she was, oblivious to the dangers around her, caring for nothing but her new kids.

The kids were not strong enough to follow their mother yet, so I would have to carry them. I picked them up by the paws, hung them over my arms, and began to make my way down the slope, through the valley-bed and up the other side of the ridge. Shamad was right on my heels, bleating as she tagged along. I was exhausted and every few yards I would stop, put down the kids, sit for a minute to catch my breath and then, lifting them up again, trudge a few more yards. I knew that I had no time to waste to catch up with Taahe, where I would leave the kids and Shamad, before setting off in search of the rest of the goat herd. If I let dusk arrive without the herd secured in their corral, the animal kingdom of carnivores would be feasting on them.

When I did not immediately find my brother and his herd of sheep, I began to fear another mishap. Trickling sweat, kids draped over each arm, and Shamad trailing behind me, I negotiated the treacherous slope.

Then I spied Taahe. Thankfully, he had already collected the sheep and was in the process of prodding them back home. As he approached me with an appearance of manufactured menace, I knew that he was going to remind me that, as head of the herdsmen, I had failed in my duty. He would not let me forget that I had committed the cardinal sin of losing half of my flock.

Until that moment, I had entertained a vacuous hope that my pride would remain intact. Now it was quite apparent there was precious little I could do but come to terms with my embarrassment. A chill rushed up my spine.

In the dry season particularly, goats are highly valued for their enviable ability to provide milk. Thus a failure to find them was not only going to be unbearably embarrassing but economically devastating.

The sun was hanging low and seemed to be racing to rest behind the imposing mountain in the west. We both knew what that meant: no time to recover the remaining members of the herd. The legacy of a disastrous day in history was looming. Whatever manhood was left in me was riding on a boat of despair, so I was desperate to find the appropriate words and at least feign a recovery attempt.

"So," he said. "That's it, I guess. I mean, what else is there to do? The sun is about to descend. The goats are nowhere around and every bastard predator is going to be on the prowl in a few...."

"Shut up," I shouted. "Shut up."

He bent down, picked up several pebbles, and randomly threw them one after the other. Then he turned to me with a look that said "get the hell out of my sight" but instead, he just said, "Why don't you try to see whether you can find them? Goats are very smart. They can outmaneuver most predators, perching on peaks where no danger can molest them. Or, they might just choose to head on home and in that case, they'll meet you half way."

He had now infused me with a bit of hope that if only I could gather the courage to go, I might meet the herd midway. I could at least show some effort.

"Taahe, you're right," I said. "I have to go and search. Take the sheep home but whatever you do, do not let our mother know about me and the missing goats!"

Taahe was not amused. "You're putting yourself in danger," he yelled. "We've already lost half of what we are worth. We are on the verge of getting into the neighborhood, the gossip gale, and you're asking me not to tell! I could try not to say a word, but how will that be possible?"

"Please, I beg you," I pleaded. "You know, I'm going to find them and bring them home. All of them!"

My brother shook his head in disgust, picked up the two kids, one in each arm, and walked away towards the sheep. Shamad, who had never before wavered in her loyalty to me, chose to trail him. Taahe moved from one wing of the sheep herd to the other, gathering them into a throng and then goading them toward home.

I waited awhile to see whether he might change his mind, to come back and collect me, but to no avail. Of course he had caught me in a violation of the herdsmen's golden law and, at the same time, recognized that dusk was ominously approaching with its menacing darkness. He was not willing to wade through the danger or wage a war with complacency. Thus he moved on, decisive.

Watching my little brother turn on his heels made me mad but forced me not to waste a precious minute. I took off and ran with such speed that I didn't notice that thorns had ripped through the flesh of my legs, leaving wounded streaks on my calves and thighs. Racing from the top of the ridge, descending into the valley, and then climbing again, I finally reached the peak where I thought that I had last heard the goats' bleats. But to my despair, not a single goat showed herself in appreciation of my valiant attempt. The silent solitude severed my serenity, so I moved about, restless, climbing one rock after another, scaling a thousand-year-old tree to extend my range of view. Nothing, nothing gave me the slightest glimmer of hope. I looked to the west and my heart sank. The sun was receding behind a hollow mountain that cast its gloomy shadow.

I hollered at the sun to slow her descent. She ignored my pleas.

With nowhere to go and with nothing else to do, I chose to stay in the thousand-year-old acacia tree. I crawled up and perched on the base of a branch that was high out of the hoodlum hyenas' reach. Watching the sun's lazy descent, my heart sank. Thick darkness fell and closed in around me. I found solace in knowing that lions were not going to maul me tonight. Lions had no ecological attachment to this high mountainous land; hyenas were too heavy to heave themselves up into my tree; human thieves were too impatient to take any interest; cheetahs were too timid to tussle with me; and jackals were too clever to waste tactical maneuvers on me. But still, the daring leopard could dispatch her demons of death.

I wrestled with what to do if disaster came. Solutions evaded me. The blanket of darkness, the howling of the jackals, the baboons that began to yowl, and the batches upon batches of bugs that bit my skin, all kept me paralyzed.

Sometime that evening, I heard my mother calling my name, "Doogle! Doogle!"

Every inch of my body was immobilized, even my voice box. I was terrified predators would hear me if I called and have me for a meal.

Her voice reverberated throughout the hollow valley. She called all night long, alternating the pitch of her voice from high to low. All I could do was muster the strength to keep myself in the tree, neither falling asleep nor muttering a word. As I heard my mother mourn, night washed me with dew. It was a merciless, slow moving night. But, as she probably intended, her distant cries kept me company, hopeful that the dawn would provide a safe return home.

Throughout the night, I suffered the savage beating of hysteria until finally daybreak dispatched the hopes that had departed with the darkness. An orange glow radiated sages of amber beauty that I had known and seen so often but never admired. Resuscitated by the sun's morning rays, my fear vanished. Within an hour of those first morning rays, I felt warmer and "wiser."

The limbs that were numb last night, the larynx that lacked the courage to cough, and the legs that were limp miraculously filled with renewed vigor and I climbed down. Once I landed on the ground, I hastened to take an inventory, checking to see whether the host tree had taken any of me for itself. Satisfied that I was whole, I hurried to my mother. Suddenly I heard her melodic voice again and melted into exuberant waves of emotional exhilaration. As soon as I saw her, I dashed forward with maddening speed and threw myself into her arms, holding on to her ever-so tightly, weeping.

It seemed ages before we both gained our composure. She released me from her embrace, held me back to stare lovingly at me before pulling me back into her again. She did that many times as though she were not convinced it was me.

"I thought I had lost you last night," she finally uttered in a hoarse voice. "Hooyo, don't ever, ever do that to me again."

"Yes, Hooyo," I responded.

"No matter what, do you hear me, Hooyo?" she asked.

"Yes, Hooyo. I will never do that again."

"Whatever else is in danger, I don't care, Hooyo. Your life is more important to me than everything we have. Do you hear me, Hooyo?" my mother repeated, wiping the tears from my face with the hem of her gown.

"Yes, Hooyo." For the first time, I savored the meaning and weight of the word *hooyo*, which means mother or my child, thus used interchangeably in Somali.

"Now, let's find those useless goats that have caused me so much grief and almost cost me my son's life. OK?"

"Yes, Hooyo," I said, surprised that she was no longer distraught nor distressed about the loss of the "precious" goats whose care she had always grumbled about.

"Where were they when you saw them last? And where the hell were you anyway?"

O, ooh, she cha-a-anged her mind, watch out, I thought.

But she checked herself. "Never mind about where you were. Just tell me where you last saw them."

Over the mountaintop, then over another and another, we finally came upon a gigantic rise fortified by cliffs and flanked by chasms. These cliffs and chasms were empowered by solid, massive rocks seated in the corners of each twist of the trail. Carved by nature, in the middle of the mountain face, was a dark cave normally inhabited by baboons and not easily accessible to the hated hyena. However, it was not a safe haven from cheetahs, jackals, man or that most ingenious cat—the leopard.

There they were, our throng of goats, chewing their cud. My mother approached, slow and cautious, as though she were invading a herd of wild gazelles. She called a few goats by their names and they responded with a friendly bleat. We waded through the flock, petting each goat in passing to show our gratitude for the reunion.

They rose and began to mill about. My mother grabbed one of the strongest he-goats by the leg but he jumped and jerked away. Getting ahold of him by the ear, she hauled him out of the cave. He leaped into the air, landed on all fours, and dashed down the slope before halting, abruptly. He appeared to give a silent signal to the rest of the herd. In a minute, they followed by twos, threes, and on and on until my mother, who was trying to make a head count, decided to restrict the flow.

"Ninety-eight, ninety-nine, hundred, hundred-one…"

I had no clue when or how she had reached the hundreds.

"…Hundred-two, three, hundred-four,….. hundred-seven, hundred-eight."

"Did I say hundred-five and six?" she asked.

"Yes, Hooyo," I said, trying not to contradict her.

"Hundred-ten, hundred-eleven, hundred-twelve," she went on, looking back, then letting some pass by.

"Hundred-thirty-seven, hundred-thirty-eight, nine. Ooh, they are all here, thank God for His mercy." She sighed as the last two goats scuttled past her.

"Or did I over count them?" she whispered to herself.

"No, no," she reassured herself, "It doesn't matter much now even if there is one or two or twenty missing. I have my son and, if not all, most of my prized goats. Thank God."

She dropped her stick and opened her arms up for me, smiling ever so gently. She clutched me so tight around the ribcage that I had to beg her to go easy. Minutes passed before she seemed satisfied. She let go, stood back, held my hand, twirled me about, pulled me to herself, held me away, then inspected me all over again before she led me out of the cave into the herd.

"Now," she ordered. "Collect them from the left, and let's get home before the children let the sheep out of the corral." She presented me with her herding stick before walking to the other side of the herd.

"*Jii, jii, jii, hoow, hoow, hoow, caa, caa,*" she howled, ordering the herd to stay tightly together as she guided them back home.

On the way back, the sky turned to azure. The eerie feeling of desolation had departed. The sound of the goats' hooves beating on the poor earth resounded like that of pouring rain. A mile away or so from our enclosure, a pack of the most despised creatures of the savannah, the hyenas, appeared in our view. We, the mother-son pair of brave souls, broke down with laughter, for we were aware of how ridiculous the hyenas looked. They had lost their opportunity to feast on our herd.

"If only they had known where to look," my mother quipped, "if only they had known where to look last night."

I laughed with exaggerated disgust at the hyenas' misfortune.

Yards from our enclosure, the rest of the family—sisters, brother Taahe, all—came, came out to greet us.

Taahe rushed toward me with an embellished pace, then suddenly came to a halt a few feet away. "Has your men's menstruation let up?" he called out for all to hear, laughing.

Then he dashed away, pairing up with Mom and, from behind her, waving at me furtively.

The Mayxaano Chronicles:
A Man of Means

It was late in the afternoon in Ceerigaabo when Bilaal and Mayxaano decided to check on Dalmar—or Dooli, as the kids called him. He was out in the soccer field—agile, as a veteran midfielder, supplying the ball to the rest of his team, high-fiving the others, laughing and running about like a rabbit.

Mayxaano and Bilaal were so impressed that they, too, high-fived each other every time he held the ball.

"There he goes. There he goes," Mayxaano repeated. She turned and left the field, beginning the walk home.

Bilaal followed her.

"Do you see how happy he is, now that he has his own ball?" she asked.

"I can't believe how a simple game of soccer can change a child's mood," he said.

"Well, one job is done: we brought Doolli—no, no, that is what the other kids call him—Dalmar's spirit back," said Mayxaano.

"Amen to that, Mayxaano. By the way, I am curious, why is that you care so much about kids?"

Mayxaano stopped and looked at Bilaal. "I am always bothered by that question. Simple, I have been there. So I try to see the world from a child's mind. At times, all a child needs is a touch of attention."

About a block or so away, the two teenagers passed a group of women gathered in front of a house. A well-dressed man goaded a donkey laden with vessels of water. He crossed the road before them and stopped at the shoulder of a solitary house. He took a vessel of water off the donkey and, carrying it with his hands, entered the house. He came out with an empty vessel, replaced it on the slot, lifted another, and repeated the process. As he was about to take a third vessel of water up to the house, Bilaal stopped to watch but Mayxaano kept on walking. About seventy feet away, she turned around. "What is so amusing about a Biyoole doing this job?"

"Why do you sound so snarky and accusatory, annunciating 'Biyoole'?" Bilaal asked. "You seem to be suggesting that there is something wrong with paying attention to a man so dignified that he dresses up even though he is selling water, the most demeaning job in Somalia."

Mayxaano forced out a chuckle and walked off.

"What in the world does that mean, Mayxaano?"

Mayxaano neither responded to his question nor stopped.

"What the hell does that mean, Mayxaano?" Bilaal yelled after her.

Mayxaano maintained her graceful gait. She was about to turn into the corner grocery store when the Biyoole came out of the house, running. In his left hand was the last empty vessel. A woman, a shoe in her hand, ran after him, apparently intending to beat him with it. She was dressed in a red diric and skirt but was bare-headed, missing the requisite headscarf.

The Biyoole dashed to the other side of the donkey. Every time the woman with the shoe tried to catch up with him, he moved to the other side of the donkey. He ran in circles around the donkey, shifting the empty jar from one hand to the other.

Another woman made out of the house closest to the woman-in-red. "*Naa Ilaahay ka yaab, naa Ilaahay ka yaab, oo ninka miskiinka ah faraha ka qaad* [Fear God, fear God and leave the poor man alone]," she yelled, placing herself between the Biyoole and the irate woman.

"This animal thinks he can outsmart me," said the woman-in-red. "I am tired of him cheating me my water service."

"What is he cheating you out of? He is eking out a living to feed his family. That does not mean that he is a mindless animal. You are the one who is cheating the poor man. You have no shame, lady. The whole neighborhood is tired of your endless charade, the way you take out your fury on this poor man."

The irate woman flew upon the other, grabbed her by the hair, and pulled her to the ground. She was about to straddle her when the Biyoole rushed over. But before he reached them, the neighbor woman slipped a hand into the irate woman's bosom and tore the red diric off her. The woman-in-red blessed the scene with her bare breasts, forcing the Biyoole to back off. But he could not leave the two entangled ladies to themselves. Averting his gaze, he walked closer and managed to grab hold of the woman-in-red. He peeled her off the other.

No sooner had he done so than the second woman jumped up and assailed them both.

Bilaal, who had been frozen in confusion, shook himself and hurried to get hold of the first woman. He was struggling to secure a hold on her when three, now four, then six women from the neighborhood all came running out of their houses. The first woman swathed a shawl over the woman-in-red. The others grabbed ahold of her and the Biyoole hastily took his leave.

The women held onto their furious neighbor and hauled her back to her house. Then they locked her inside.

The neighborhood women convened a meeting right outside the woman-in-red's house. Some were outraged that she had dared to be indifferent to her indecency, others were furious that she had made a habit out of assaulting the Biyoole, and still others fanned the flame.

"She has no shame. Her breasts were flying free for all eyes to feast on and she did not manage an iota of sense to attend to them. My God, what kind of woman would disgrace herself so openly in public?" asked one.

"She is a lunatic with no logic at all. And worse yet, she has been taking advantage of this poor man since the day she arrived in the neighborhood," another added.

"She is a vulture. She takes advantage of the weak and vulnerable," one chimed in.

"She is not the only party to be blamed here," one countered. "Why does he patronize her to begin with? He should not sell a cup of water to her if she is not paying for it."

"You are kidding, right," another confronted her. "He is eking out a living. He cannot abandon the whole neighborhood because of her. Besides, he may be afraid that others in the neighborhood will side with her, causing him to lose his customer base."

"I hope he knows how we feel about her. He should not let her take advantage of him," lamented yet another.

The cluster of women did not notice Bilaal standing next to them, listening. He was trying his best to make sense out of the brawl; but eventually, he concluded it was best to move on.

Bilaal passed by Saalax Xaaji Xasan's house, pushed ahead and marveled at Jibriil Xaaji Ducaale's mansion. Another block on, he turned right at Ina-maatan's shop where Axmed Kuutiye's legendary blue truck was unloading sacks of rice for Ina-mataan. Sand dust was caked all over the hood.

He dipped a forefinger in the sand dust, examining it as though he were a sage and could determine where in Somalia it was attained.

"Hey," someone called out from the top of the truck bed. "What can I do for you?"

"I am wondering where you contracted this type of sand dust," said Bilaal as it occurred to him it was the Kirishbey.

"You are telling me that you are a sand dust expert?" the Kirishbey asked.

"No, I just wanted to know what kind of sand dust stays caked on the body of a truck with such fidelity."

"Boy, you need to learn a lot about your country, I would say. Have you ever been to Saraar? You should know that is where the sun feels lonely and the wind has nowhere to rest. In other words, the land is so bare that if a single tree were to be placed there, it would shed tears of mercy for life. There, once the sand dust hears an engine roaring, it stands up because it, too, wants to leave. So it clings to the trucks that are unfortunate enough to run through it."

Bilaal was about to follow up with another question when, from the corner of his eye, he caught Mayxaano approaching. "You're back. What was with you, anyway? You left a scene where a crime was about to take place, Mayxaano."

"I am not the police, am I?" she snapped.

"No, but you could have helped."

"Easy for you to say. You don't live here. We do! You are going to leave for your cozy Mogadishu soon. You have no idea what social dirt is buried beneath this squabble."

"What kind of social dirt? What are you hinting at, Mayxaano?"

"One that your kind has neither the ears to hear nor the eyes to see, Bilaal."

"My kind? Now you are insulting me."

"Insulting you; no, I am not insulting you. You are insulting yourself."

"How?"

"There are heaps of social dirt that your people choose not to know about yet perpetually benefit from."

"Your people, who is the 'your people' that you referring to? Why don't you address me, not the 'your people' you are talking about? Go ahead, Mayxaano, please enlighten me."

"Enlighten you, enlighten you, Bilaal. I am tired of the self-righteousness that all of you are born into. I am tired of this clan privilege that you have been taught to live off, so much that you make sure that you don't stand on your own legs but on other people's, that…"

"Hold it, hold it, Mayxaano, please!"

"Please don't interrupt me. I am trying to enlighten you as you asked, Sir."

"I, I, I…"

"Yeah, 'I, I, I.' See, you can't take it when it is offered to you, can you?"

"Please, don't speak for me," said Bilaal.

"Why the fuck do you think that I am speaking for you? I am speaking for myself, Sir, if you can believe it. Now, this conversation is over." And with that, she walked off.

"Mayxaano, Mayxaano," he called after her. "Please."

Dejected, Bilaal turned the other way and went home. On his way, as he talked to himself, a stray, hungry dog whimpered at him.

"Hey, your language is so much clearer than that of human beings," he said to the dog. "Are you that hungry?" He bent over, trying not to touch him. Most Muslims believe that dogs are unclean and avoid patting them or touching their saliva.

"OK, OK, you have to wait for me here," he said. "I am going to steal some leftover meat from my aunt. Would that be OK with you?"

The dog wagged his tail.

"Come to think of it, I will not be able to steal meat for you. You know that is the main meal in this land. So, I am going to be in trouble if I do that. But I have a few pennies. I am going to get you a loaf of bread from Raanguuri's bakery. You realize his bread is sought after."

The dog whimpered.

"OK, OK, you are telling me to be quiet, aren't you? I got it. You are right, my man. Just wait here." Bilaal rushed home. He went straight to the kitchen. He looked around, found some leftover rice, and came back out with a bowl. But the dog was already gone.

"Man," he sighed. "I thought I was going to feel useful. I cannot seem to do anything right today."

Heartsick, he went to his room. He took off his shoes, his shirt and pants, put his macawis on, and took a nap.

About an hour later, Xariir pulled the blanket off. "Bilaal, you are late. We have been waiting for you for thirty minutes."

Bilaal did not move.

"I am talking to you. This is unlike you, Bilaal. Why do you look so sad? Did anything happen?"

Bilaal did not answer.

"I am talking to you. Are you OK?"

"Is Mayxaano there?" asked Bilaal

"Yes, but she was late, too. What is with you two tonight? The kids are waiting for us."

Bilaal was slow to raise his head. He sat on the edge of the bed and wiped his eyes with his right hand. "I will be there in a minute."

"Hurry please. You know they are always eager to see you both," Xariir said.

"Yeah, they are always eager to see Mayxaano," Bilaal whispered.

He looked in the mirror and ran his fingers through his curly hair, quickly refreshing himself before he went next door.

He was greeted with applause. That cheered him a bit. Before taking a seat, he looked where he expected Mayxaano to be. She had changed from her usual seat and was sitting in the corner, out of his direct view. She must still be mad. He wondered why in the world she felt so harassed.

Once the lessons for the kids began, the serious matter in front of them suppressed their side anger. Bilaal marveled how Mayxaano always arrested the children's attention through her reading of *The Thousand and One Nights*, which she had to translate into Somali as she read the Arabic version. As usual, when she opened her mouth, not a soul made a sound.

But throughout the session, Mayxaano avoided looking at Bilaal.

Bilaal was relieved when he heard Xariir tell the children, "Hey, young people, that is it for tonight. Go home, eat, sleep, and get ready for tomorrow."

"Aaaaaaaah," the children protested.

"Come on, you guys. Is that how we thank Mayxaano? Let us say it all at once. One, two, threeee…"

"A mile closer tonight but another to go tomorrow," cheered the children, their motto to conclude.

"There we go," said Xariir. "See you all tomorrow, *insha'Allah*. Make sure you take your exercise books with you."

"Thanks, guys. I love each and every one of you in a special way," Mayxaano said, hugging each student on his or her way out.

After the children cleared the room, the house became quiet. An awkward silence seemed to linger.

Mayxaano walked to the door, opened it slowly, and stepped out.

Bilaal followed Mayxaano out the door and down the street. He wasn't sure what he intended but he couldn't let her leave like this, still angry. Yet he couldn't bring himself to catch up with her. When she slowed her steps, he slowed down to keep the distance between them.

About half a mile later, she stopped and turned around. "If you keep on following me but aren't man enough to address me, I should be 'the man' to ask what is on your mind. Obviously, it is not that urgent of a matter to you, I can tell," she said.

He approached her. "First, you don't have to be a man to address me. You can remain your beautiful, gentle self and much smarter than any man I know. Second, I just want you to talk to me."

"OK, OK." Mayxaano sighed. "At least you found the right words. Listen, Bilaal, there is a major social sickness and dirt in Somali society. As a matter of fact, I know it's not your fault but I am not sure whether taking it out on you is not fair. After all you are a part of the privileged class…"

"What privileged class are you talking about?" interrupted Bilaal.

"See, that is why I am not able to have a conversation with your kind. I give up. I give up." She threw her hands in the air and walked away.

"Mayxaano, stop, stop, please."

She continued to walk. He was losing her.

"Mayxaano, Mayxaano, I beg you, please stop."

Mayxaano put her arms across her chest, and stared.

"Listen, I am so sorry, I am going to keep quiet. I am, please. I promise."

"OK, you have one chance. And if you screw this one up, I will never, never talk to you. Is that clear?"

He did not answer.

"See, you are not really ready." She motioned as if she was going to start walking again.

He placed himself right in front of her. "No, please, I am ready, serious. It's just your threat that frightens me. At least allow me a margin of error with the ultimatum."

"No. I have been living with a margin of error all my life and you think you have the right to use it for a negotiation ploy?"

"Mayxaano, forget it. I take that back. No margin of error. Now, please, go on."

Mayxaano sighed. She straightened her body and looked around, then turned to face him.

"Go ahead, man it?" said Bilaal, using a Somali phrase that means toughen up.

"Man it, man it. Do you hear yourself, Bilaal?"

"My God, I am not going to win this, am I?"

"Again, your patronizing behavior is baffling. You see your language, 'Man it, I am not going to win.' All your vocabulary is about summoning superiority over a perceived weakness. Let me tell you something. Whoever is on a perpetual war for status is the weakest of mankind. He is fearful that he is going to lose his artificially inflated social rank."

"OK, OK, we are in the sixties. Obviously, America has arrived in the Horn of African with its feminist fever. Sure, let me remind you what you left out, the sexual revolution?" said Bilaal.

"Oh, I forgot; you Somali men are denying me my existence but adoring my sexuality. What a contradiction."

"Aw, man, aw, man. Mayxaano, can you listen to me? That is not what I meant."

"Yeah, what did you mean exactly? Because all I know is that you walked yourself into a trap with your eyes wide open."

"Man, listen…"

"No, you listen, Bilaal. And if you do, you might, I stress might, learn a thing or two tonight. No, no, I take that back. I can't get through to you." And finally, she walked off.

"Mayxaano, Mayxaano, please, I, I…"

She kept walking.

"I think I am in love with this woman," he said so softly that he almost didn't hear himself speak. "No, I know I am. Mayxaano, please!" And he ran after her.

"If you keep chasing me, can we at least go somewhere to sit? This city talks, you know. No decent girl should be out with the opposite sex this time of night. You do know that, don't you?"

"Mayxaano, I do want to listen. So you tell me, where should we go?"

"There, there, Bilaal. That is the kind of question I can answer. My mother is away. I should warn you though that my uncle is due to arrive anytime. But we probably have enough time to address some facts."

"When is he going to arrive?" asked Bilaal.

"I will let you know ahead of time. Anyway, if we are going to use my house, I should also make you aware that it is not anything like the mansion you live in. It's a roof over our heads, OK?"

Bilaal smiled. "Mayxaano, I am not interested in the house or the look of it. I am interested in what you have to tell me. And," he hesitated, "you."

"Don't say that you were not told," she warned him.

They walked to her house in silence. She opened the door,

stepped aside, and let him into the living room.

"There, please have a seat," she said. "I am going to bring you a cup of tea."

Bilaal could not help but scan the room. "No, no, Mayxaano, please. I am not able to wait for the tea. I just want to…"

"Fine, Bilaal, since you are so hell-bent to prove me wrong…"

"Ha…" Bilaal opened his mouth.

"Ah, ah. You better not. Remember the warning."

He pointed to his lips and made a sign that they were sealed. He motioned as though he were throwing the key away.

"It's about time," Mayxaano said. "On second thought, you better get that key to your mouth back, because I may need you to say something when I am done."

Again, he pointed to his lips and made the same sign.

"Why am I enjoying this?" She smiled. "Anyway, let me tell you about the dirt that has been buried beneath the veil that you have refused to see. You refused to know because you were born into a privileged clan status. And while you are at it, you have been wiping your waste on us. Do you know that? By the way, you can answer that question." She took a seat next to him.

"No. I have no idea what you are talking about, Mayxaano."

"Good. I didn't think you would. But I admire you admitting it. Let me educate you. Privilege means when you live such a sheltered life, you don't know what harm you afflict on others. Let me ask you this, Bilaal, do you know anything about Somalia's clan caste system? Do you know the social, psychological crime that many Somalis suffer from?"

"Matter of fact, I thought… never mind. I am listening," said Bilaal.

"I am telling you, Bilaal, you have no idea what that is like if you have not lived it."

"Maybe you are right because..."

"I know I am right, damn it. I am living it, Bilaal. I am living it." She stood up and paced back and forth in the living room. "I am one of thousands who are living with a sour shame and pain. I am living psychological trauma and torture. I face it every hour of the day, three hundred sixty five days of the year, Bilaal. Do you hear me? Do, you heaaaaaaaaaar me, Bilaal? You call me 'Midgaan.' You call me 'Midgaan.'"

Bilaal stood up, walked to the window, came back, sat again and just stared at her.

"Aw, wait, wait," she said and took a seat. "Wait, now that you know that I am a 'plague,' will I lose you? I may never see you again, Bilaal. So before I contaminate your pure, precious clan pedigree by simply talking about a social disease, please run."

"Please go on, tell me what I need to hear." Bilaal hung his head low and looked at the floor.

"Wow, I am surprised that you are still here."

"Mayxaano, please, would you? I have been a witness to a sort of colonial caste system in Kenya so I am not completely insensitive. But go on."

"What I will let you know," she said, "is a secret so sacred that since we came to Ceerigaabo eleven years ago from Yemen, no one breathed a whiff of it but between the three of us." She paused. "The three of us are my mother, my uncle, and me. In fact, my uncle is married to my mother. Thank God my mother has not gotten pregnant to expose us all. You don't understand how a social diet of daily humiliation can muscle you into submission. Now, let me ask you this, how would you feel if you were related to the man you saw being humiliated in the height of the day in the middle of the street for all to see? If he were married to your mother but in secret, if he were your uncle but can't tell a soul, and if he comes home but only in the dead of night or with an excuse for a few minutes, how would that make you feel?"

"What? You don't say, Mayxaano. Don't tell me that..."

"Yeah, Bilaal, who do you think the uncle I am talking about is? " She quieted down. Bilaal could sense that she was holding her tears of anger back. Her jaws were moving mechanically. "Yes, I am telling you that man is my flesh and blood uncle. My paternal uncle. Your kind called him 'Midgaan,' Bilaal. So was my father. And I, a descendant of them, I am called the same name."

Bilaal was now holding his tears back. He felt shamed— shamed for her, shamed for himself.

"It gets more complicated, Bilaal. My mother isn't 'Midgaan.' My mother is what you guys call 'Aji' or 'Nasab,' whatever term that satisfies your vanity at the moment. The Somali world 'Aji' is not strong enough for your claim so your people had to borrow an Arabic word, 'Nasab,' pure pedigree."

"Mayxaano, how have you managed to live with that kind of weight?" He slipped his hands into his pants pockets, staring at her. "Well, how could anyone?" he asked himself.

"Just like you, I was born in Yemen, a city called Ra's Sharwayn at the edge of the Gulf of Aden. My father and mother were the only Somalis there. They got married. Six years later when I was five, my father was bitten by a snake. He died soon after."

"How did they end up there? Do you know?"

"My mother was working for a British anthropologist at the time. My father had left his nomad family, went to a small town of Xiis, and hid himself in the belly of a boat loaded with sheep and headed to Aden. He was thirteen. The boat capsized on the way. People believed that there were no survivors but my father swam to shore and was found by fishermen. One of them, a good man, volunteered to take him home, nursed him back to life, and taught him how to read the Holy Quran. He learned Arabic and arithmetic. Soon he became a man of letters, I am told. He earned his respect, grew larger and larger in the community. Not long after, in his early twenties, he became a man of means, an administrator.

"He was no longer a 'Midgaan' but a respected leader in that small town. There he lost the cursed identity. Ironically, he was still known as The-Somali-off-the-sea. When my mother fell in love with him, he had told her who he was to Somalis and that her family would disown her if she married him. My mother said she did not care. She was so in love with him that she was going to make him her husband, regardless. My mother said to me, 'Ah, Hooyo, he was so handsome and smart. I was not going to leave that kind of man to any other woman.'

"He told my mother that one of his brothers was selling water off a donkey, a Biyoole in Ceerigaabo last time he had heard. When my mother came here, the first person she secretly sought out was my uncle, the Biyoole. It turned out that he was a very, very wise man. He is the one who advised my mother not to reveal my identity until I am old enough to decide for myself. 'At least,' he said, 'she does not have to face the double jeopardy of being called "Midgaan" as well as the daughter of a Biyoole uncle which in itself is the lowest of the low in Somali social status.' They agreed that I shouldn't acknowledge him in public lest our emotions betray us both. That was why I was neither able to withstand the public humiliation he suffered today nor was I any kind of help.

"He also told my mother not to reveal their marriage either, again because of me. And that no one should know that the

'Midgaan' is married to 'a pure' pedigree, my mother. As I said earlier, he comes home in the dead of night. If he comes in the daylight, he pretends that he is delivering water to our house.

"There you have it. That is my life story and you are going to carry the burden of that secret with you, Bilaal. Now you are the only person who knows besides the three of us."

When Mayxaano paused, Bilaal stood up. He held both of her hands in his and stared into her eyes. Looking at her, he could feel the innocent, tender heart that had borne all the horror of the Somali caste system. Slowly, he pulled her into an embrace and landed a kiss on her lips. She allowed it to linger. Gently, she pushed him away, warning that her uncle might walk in on them at any moment.

Bilaal walked out the front door. He looked back and extended his hand to her. She took it into hers and lifted it onto her heart, right above her breast.

Bilaal stepped back, keeping his eyes on Mayxaano. He took another step and then another. Then he turned around and walked away, increasing his pace faster and faster until he was sprinting.

He was elated beyond belief that he had kissed Mayxaano, his first kiss ever. In seconds, though, the weight of her sadness and the power of the secret she had entrusted to him slowed him down. He could hear her saying, "Now you are the only person who knows besides the three of us."

Her story forced him to think back. He saw that he had been guilty of causing the same pain she had endured. Though he had never insulted Mayxaano, he had hurt one of his childhood friends in Kenya, a Kikuyu boy, when he was nine years old. He had heard the white staff of a segregated school for Asians and Somalis using the "N" word against other black employees. A few days later, Bilaal himself had used the same

"N" word to refer to his own friend. Now he felt attacked by the weight of how much he had hurt his Kenyan friend.

For the first time his life, he equated the word "Midgaan" with the "N" word. He wondered whether anybody had heard him when he assaulted his own friend with it. He wondered if his use of the word had permitted others to wield it against his friend, too.

The Mayxaano Chronicles:
Don't Lose

Haybe, a certified accountant, was in his office in Hartford, Connecticut when the telephone rang. He looked at the pile of paperwork that he had to go through before he was set to leave at 4:30 on Friday afternoon. It was his first professional job since he had arrived from Somalia eight years previously. A high school dropout who made it through college with sheer determination, Haybe loved his paycheck. He rejoiced in the fact that he was able to answer phone calls in the dead of night from one relative or the other stranded somewhere around the globe. And there was no end to it. Just the other day his cousin called from Kenya. What city, he did not ask but he knew the problem was urgent. And what else would he ask for but money to save his five children and wife? A month ago, it was his friend in Yemen. He was sick in a refugee camp. Within the same week, it was his gregarious classmate in Moscow. He was desperate for a train ticket out of Moscow to anywhere. Haybe guessed anywhere meant to Scandinavia or the UK but who knew?

Who could blame them? Since the Hargeisa student uprising in 1982 had morphed into civil war, which exploded in 1990, Somalis were leaving their country in droves.

Haybe knew how fortunate he was. He had left before the exodus of thousands of his fellow countrymen had begun. For sure though, Haybe was not happier, for he was concerned about his family's safety. But at least he could afford to feed them through the Hawala money wiring system.

There were problems. Haybe hated his job. Three out of seven of his colleagues complained about their spouses, another two about everything and anything in life. One had a bad case of burping sonorously loudly on the telephone. The only sane person that he got along with was "the-mother-of-two-dogs," as she liked to call herself. But the-mother-of-two-dogs would only talk if someone was willing to listen to long stories about her two dogs. There were occasions that if one were lucky, one would be able to lure her away from her habit. On these occasions, she was witty and funny.

When Haybe did not answer, the caller hung up but soon called back. Once more, Haybe ignored the ringing phone, picked up a cluster of papers, and began to calculate how he could manage to go home on time. Again, the caller hung up and called back again. Annoyed, he reached for the receiver and picked up and yelled in Somali, "*Maxaad naga rabtaa* [What do you want?]" In fact he had no clue whether the caller spoke Somali but he was so irritated that he said what was in his mind.

"Good God; you have not changed an inch," the caller said. "How rude of you! Is that how you answer the phone? What if I were your boss? Hold it, hold it. Don't answer that. I know, I know you knew that you were safe under the Somali language shadow." The caller chuckled. The chuckling lingered.

Haybe's mind fussed over the mystery caller's chuckle for a second. "Raage, is that you?"

"Why? Did you send your tribesman to silence me? If you did, you better get your money back because you can see that they missed me by a mile. How incompetent of them. The proof is that I am here talking you," said Raage.

"Man, aw, man. How the hell are you, Brother? I have to

tell you, I might have sent my henchman on your way, but I am glad to hear your voice today. On a more serious note, tell me, how long have you been here?"

"I am calling from Toronto, Haybe, been here for three months now. Boy, do I have a ton of tales to tell you. But first, how the hell are you, too?"

"I am fine, I am fine, but I want to hear you out."

"Man, how much time do you have?"

Haybe looked at the clock and realized he had just 45 minutes before he could go home. He looked away and rested his eyes on the pile of paperwork on his desk waiting for him before the end of the day. That Raage was a master storyteller whose ability to tailor any tale to his own reality tortured him. If Raage started, he would have no time to escape home. But he needed to know about his hometown: schoolmates, neighbors, the landscape after the civil war. He heard himself say, "We have a bit of time before I go home."

"Assuming that all is well with you, Haybe, let me ask you, do you really want to hear it all?" Raage asked.

"Yes, I do want to hear it all. When were you last in our hometown?"

"I left Ceerigaabo six months ago."

"And you have been there throughout the war?"

"Yes. Most of it anyway. And Haybe, let me tell you, what happened in our city has never been seen in Somalia's history nor has it been imagined."

"How so?" Haybe asked.

"Let me tell you..."

Raage began to relate how their hometown turned on each other: neighbor against neighbor, paternal cousin against maternal, uncle against nephew, teacher against student, classmate against class, and on and on. With his oratorical skills, Raage unleashed layers of losses: loss of innocence, loss of property, loss of faith, loss of identity, and, worst of all, loss of lives. He went on to list the names of people murdered and who murdered them. As he was going through his recitation, Haybe began to write down the names he recognized. He began to feel a nauseating pain. He wanted Raage to stop talking but how could he seem so insensitive? How could he sound like a soulless native son? The lugubrious narratives nibbled his mind. Haybe put up with it until Raage dropped one name: Dalmar.

"Hold it, hold it," he screamed. "Did you say Dalmar? Dalmar was among the casualties? The same Dalmar that led us to our first regional tournament championship in 1978?"

"Yes, he was among the causalities."

Haybe felt himself drift into space. The receiver dropped from his grip as he began to remember the last soccer game that his friend Dalmar had played. He had been there that day. He remembered it like it was yesterday.

On May 27, 1978, at 3:30 in the afternoon, the entire city of Burco, young and old, was pouring into Burco Soccer Stadium, where that afternoon Sanaag and Waqooyigalbeed Region were facing off.

On this special day, an exhilarating competitive spirit lifted the air. It was the last day of the Regional Sports Tournament in the northern part of Somalia, hosted this year by the splendid city of Burco. Two teams had sworn to face off against one another, and the winner of that contest would accompany the Burco team from Togdheer Region, which, having already secured its place in the second leg of the tournament, was preparing for the trip to the capital city of Mogadishu, to complete the race for the championship.

Countless fans of the Waqooyigalbeed team had rented buses and organized into carpools to make what they called the "Good Omen Trip" from Hargeisa, the capital city of Waqooyigalbeed Region, to Burco. Their intention was to provide all the pandemonium and noise they could muster to help their team win and send the team from Sanaag home in the agony of defeat.

When you are poked, you sprint into action. And by the time the Hargeisa caravans had left for Burco on their Good Omen Trip, the Sanaag fans had already been tipped off that Waqooyigalbeed was on the way. So the Sanaag fans organized a counterattack and called it the "Don't Lose Organization." They spread the news that Waqooyigalbeed was coming to everyone they could reach in and around Burco, and stressed that it was the duty of everyone in Togdheer to support its old neighboring city's team. They reminded people that Sanaag used to be a part of Togdheer before acquiring its own autonomy, and that the poor Sanaag fans, unlike those from Waqooyigalbeed, had not been able to make the long, dusty, arduous trip from Sanaag's capital, Ceerigaabo, to Burco on the terrible dirt road that ran between the two, while the men from Hargeisa were able to get off the buses with their shirts as white as when they had first put them on back home and the women got off with their facial cream still glowing on their cheeks. The Waqooyigalbeed fans would even be able to share their elation with each other in the afternoon and still get home in time for a musical at the Hargeisa National Theatre that night!

As the old Somali saying goes, "A teacher who inspires a student today takes the risk of being outshone by him tomorrow." So the people from Hargeisa had provoked the people from Burco to storm the stadium in support of the Sanaag soccer team. At the start of the game, not an inch of the floor, much less a single seat, was vacant. If you had thrown a stick in the air, it would not have landed on the ground.

Despite all this support, within the first 15 minutes, the Sanaag team fell victim to the voracity of Waqooyigalbeed's relentless attack. First one goal was scored by Waqooyigalbeed; then, a few minutes later, another. The sudden slap in the face made the Sanaag fans soften their chanting and subdue their drums. The score was 2 for Waqooyigalbeed, 0 for Sanaag.

While all this was going on around him, one man stood silently, keenly taking it all in. Dalmar, at 16, was not only the youngest member of Sanaag's team but the youngest of all those gathered to compete. A young man with well-developed muscles and God-given talent for soccer, Dalmar had sharpened his skills through hours of feverish solitary practice. It was no accident that so many fans admired him for both his ability and his love for the game.

Dalmar had not yet played a single minute in the tournament. He was glued to the bench because his coach feared he was too young to face fierce competitors who would not hesitate to use the advantage of age and experience to crush his bones on the field. So Dalmar had to watch the game from his cruel seat on the bench—and with a song that had captivated his mind burning in his heart. He had heard the song at least a thousand times since the tournament began, especially as the Radio Hargeisa mobile truck had passed through the neighborhood where he was staying.

The famous, endlessly evocative song droned on:

I dare you, too

Whoever loses is a fool

Especially when his team was lagging behind, like now, the melody gnawed at his stomach and burned his insides.

Yet he could not remember a time when his team had been ahead—not, at any rate, since Ceerigaabo had become the capital of the newly created region of Sanaag.

Though the first half of the game seemed to drag on forever for Dalmar, after 47 minutes the referee finally blew the whistle for halftime. Each team left the field, heading off toward the side where their fans were waving flags and beating drums. But at the time, it seemed to Dalmar that Hargeisa's ebullient waving flags and beating drums were everywhere. The orchestral sound of women's ululations blending in with the men's harmonious chants took Dalmar to another world. He was imagining what it would be like to feel what the Hargeisa fans were feeling—what it would be like to be on the winning team.

Suddenly the Radio Hargeisa truck began once again to blast the melodic tune that filled him with such a mixture of sadness and joy—the sadness that smothers your spirit when your team is behind and the joy that lifts it when your team is leading.

Braves meeting for a match
On a full moon and facing off

This painful tune and Cabdicasiis Sheekh Ismaaciil (Cabdicasiis-Daqarre's) incisive lyrics filled Dalmar with sadness. He could not bear to see his team defeated, his fans disappointed, his city whipped.

The halftime seemed to take a century and a half.

Dalmar had hoped the coach might let him at least put his feet on the field, if only for a few minutes, so he could make use of his two legs and whatever aid God might lend him to avoid going home in contemptible defeat. Now he was desperately trying to think of a way to persuade his coach to let him play the rest of the game. But his hope evaporated as he realized that he could not come up with a fresh idea that would convince the coach.

Eventually the second half got under way without Dalmar. After 19 minutes, whatever hope remained in the hearts of the Sanaag fans was sucked out of them as Waqooyigalbeed assertively put the third goal into Sanaag's net.

Now the minutes were ticking away, with only 20 left before the end of the game. People had already started leaving the stadium in groups, first by twos and threes, then by tens and dozens. The desire to win had all but drained out of the Sanaag fans when a feeble voice in the middle of what was left of Sanaag's throng began to call out: "We want Dalmar, we want Dalmar, we want Dalmar." Within less than a minute, the whole stadium was reverberating with "We want Dalmar, we want Dalmar, we want Dalmar." Even the Waqooyigalbeed fans mockingly joined in, implying that it hardly mattered who got on the field to play now.

Later on, reliable sources reported that the persuasive, potent voice belonged to Mayxaano, a popular Sheikh High School teacher who was in town for the game. And though she had left Ceerigabo 10 years or so ago, never to return, Ceerigaabo never left her heart. She had sowed a seed of love there by tutoring neglected, poor neighborhood children. Dalmar, the star of the game that she was fortunate to watch, was one of the pool of children in whom she had invested.

Later on, reliable sources reported that the feeble voice belonged to Bahsan, a young lady from Boosaaso visiting relatives, who had been fortunate enough to see Dalmar practice with his teammates on several occasions. The grace and agility Dalmar displayed in these practice sessions mesmerized Bahsan. From then on, though the others came to see anyone and everyone in a Sanaag uniform, she came back to see Dalmar.

Now the Sanaag coach realized the chanting that a few seconds ago had seemed to come from no more than 10 mouths had become a resonant, rolling thunder: "We want Dalmar, we want Dalmar, we want Dalmar." Since the team would be boarding the bus soon enough for the hard, dirty trip back home, the coach supposed he might as well satisfy the fans and let Dalmar in for a while. He stood up and waved at Dalmar from the far corner of the bench, signaling for him to get into the game this instant, without the slightest warm-up. Dalmar leaped to his feet as the coach grabbed a strip of cardboard with a substitute number on it, and the two made their way straight out to the field of play.

When the nearest flag referee saw the coach from Sanaag with a cardboard number and Dalmar beside him jumping up and down, his arm shot up to flag the head referee's attention. Though the head referee caught the signal, he ignored it until the ball was kicked out of bounds, and only then, before the throw-in, did he signal for Dalmar to come into the game.

It didn't take long for Dalmar to make contact with the ball. He was still in the middle of the field and out of position when it met him midair. With his God-given talent, he seized the moment and used his chest to control the ball's ricochet. The ball rolled down his chest to the ground like water falling from a slope. Dalmar turned around and faced the enemy line like a tiger with a fresh kill. Numbers 6 and 10 of the Waqooyigalbeed team ran up to intimidate him, trying to take the ball away, but he effortlessly evaded them and smoothly passed the ball to Number 10 of his own team, who raced up toward Waqooyigalbeed's goal, then passed it off to his Number 7. Number 7 rushed on toward the goal, running parallel to the right corner of the penalty box, then cross-kicked to the penalty line, where Dalmar lay in wait. Straddling the boundary line of the penalty box, he jumped four feet in the air for the ball and simultaneously turned to meet its velocity while lying sideways in the empty air, redirecting its acceleration with the force of his kick toward the Waqooyigalbeed goal. The goalkeeper had no chance to react before the ball danced back and forth behind him, trapped in his net.

The beauty of Sanaag's first goal brought fans and foes alike to their feet. Dalmar's instant brilliant attack had given the Sanaag fans hope, energized their drums, and put an incessant exultant chant back into their mouths. All through the stadium, speculation ran riot as to whether anyone had ever seen a goal scored like this, in the Burco stadium or anywhere else.

Five minutes later, Sanaag had control again, and Dalmar received the ball from his teammate, Number 9. He dashed toward the Waqooyigalbeed defense, commanding the ball with his feet. Number 3 of Waqooyigalbeed, a huge man, rushed toward him. Dalmar calmly feinted left, then shifted right when Number 3 tried to block, leaving him in the dust. He did the same with Number 4, leaving only two of Waqooyigalbeed's defense facing him, numbers 2 and 5. As the two closed in on Dalmar, he slipped between them and passed the ball to his Number 9, who was wide open and, in another second, looked on triumphantly as the ball kissed the Waqooyigalbeed net.

Now the game had come back to life. The resuscitated fans leaped to their feet. Men threw off their turbans, women let loose their veils, and the drums clogged the stadium with a sound that, when blended with the women's ululations, seemed like an African-Arabian orchestra, churning out a European opera. As if that weren't pandemonium enough, people out on the street who'd heard the excitement over the radio, including those who'd left the game early, were now swarming over the gates and climbing the walls to get in.

From the way Sanaag had been handling the game, it was clear to the fans that it was only a matter of seconds before their team would tie it. And if it ended in a tie, Sanaag would go on to the second leg of the tournament, since in the overall scoring they had more goals than Waqooyigalbeed. The fans were right about not having long to wait. Like a cheetah pouncing from its hiding place, Dalmar sprinted out and seized the ball from the Waqooyigalbeed defense, lost in the havoc of its uncertain spin. From within that cloud, the defense stumbled on each other in a daze as Dalmar, from within the penalty box, aimed a deadly 90-degree-angle kick at the Waqooyigalbeed goal, pasting the ball against the net.

Three minutes later, the referee's whistle blew the music of the game's last breath.

The fans blindly poured on to the field and spread out, searching for Dalmar as if he were a diamond lost in the dust. But it was too late for most, because the first wave of the mob had already taken custody of him. They held and tossed him high, yet handled him with precious care as a priceless, delicate crystal, and carried him out of the stadium.

After having three goals scored against them in the last 20 minutes, Waqooyigalbeed had been obliterated. History had been made today; a new era was about to dawn in which Sanaag was going to be crowned.

Haybe awoke with a strange feeling. He heard people laughing. *No one in my office would have this much fun*, he thought. Something was not right.

A nurse walked in. "Good afternoon," she said.

"Where am I?" Haybe asked.

"You're in the hospital. You were brought in a day ago around 7:30 p.m."

"What happened?"

"You walked out of your office and into incoming traffic. You were hit by a speeding car. The report says that you flew ten feet into the air and landed on your back. You were unconscious with a concussion when the ambulance arrived."

The last he knew he was watching a soccer game!

"Wait a minute," said Haybe.

He sat up. For the first time in his adult life that he could remember, he let loose, weeping. It occurred to him that his entire memory of that last soccer game, which had seemed so vivid, had been only in his head. He must have walked out of his office in a reverie.

He remembered nothing more about how the telephone call had ended.

The Mayxaano Chronicles:
A Thorn in the Sole

At 26 and a half, Mayxaano was already a revered writer, though many people reviled her, too. She debated with men about politics, philosophy, and religion with gusto. She wore her hair loose, without the Muslim headscarf. She ran track and field, leaving most men in the dust, and, worst of all, it was rumored that she dared to write critical articles about the repressive regime in Somalia in newspapers abroad. Women vilified her publicly yet admired her privately. Men of all shades, however, stumbled over each other to have her attention for a minute.

Seventeen-year-old Ayaanle, who knew that she was not able to ignore it all, was confident that she would not let it shade her judgment on who her real friends were. He, as a close friend of hers, told her that during the summer recess, he was going back to their hometown Ceerigaabo and would make sure he would bring back all he would learn that she had missed in the last 10 years or so that she had been away: how much their neighborhood had grown, how many families had moved away, who had died, who had married, who had become rich by scamming others, and whatever else in between.

She called him one day and suddenly asked what was new. After all, she was aware that he did not have that much to share. He was a member of Sheikh High School Writing Club and she was on the advisory board; he was an "A" student and she was the best Somali language and literature teacher; he was 17-years-old and she was, you know, 26 and a half! After meticulously choosing her words, Mayxaano told him that she was willing to "mentor" him. In what, she did not say.

Of course, Ayaanle had no clue of what she was going to mentor him in, yet he was not willing to guess, lest it would abate the anticipated delight.

He knew that she was married to her poetry books and math. He thought he knew her past too; yet there was something about her that remained masked. A mystery he couldn't discern.

At 2:00 p.m. on Monday of the following week, Ayaanle had already forgotten about their encounter when classes were let out at the end of the day. Like an army of locusts, teachers and students poured out, descending on the unprotected grass with a vengeance. The distinctive, legendary uniform of white shirts and khaki pants, worn by the secondary school students, conjured up heartfelt adoration from all corners of life, for they were a source of pride for Somalis. It was said that the soil, the trees, and the meadows that they harassed with their trampling were tolerant of the inadvertent neglect. And though the abuse would make it easier for the wind to blow off the rich soil on the land between the small town of Sheikh and the two schools (the intermediate and the secondary), no one seemed to mind at all.

Ayaanle watched Mayxaano cat-walk an imaginary fashion runway obvious to her but invisible to the throng of men flanking her as soon as the bell had rung, signaling the end of the school day. She walked with a graceful firmness, taking one step at a time—not too fast, not too slow, and without too much panache. Teachers and students alike were vying for her attention when she suddenly veered to the left, emerging from the herd of men that had been gallivanting around her.

He—with his friends—did not want to transfer all the attention on her to himself. In his heart of hearts, though he appreciated her guarded interest, he didn't want it paraded in front of everyone else!

"Oh my God, is she coming for me?" he whispered to himself. Realizing that she was in fact heading towards him, he tried to trot out of the way.

Suddenly, she called him on it: "Ayaanle, please wait for me."

Ayaanle stopped and looked around, as if wondering whether there were other Ayaanles behind him. But Mayxaano did not let him hide.

"You are my Ayaanle, are you not?" she asked. "I don't care much for the other Ayaanles."

A bit embarrassed, Ayaanle managed to turn around hesitantly, as his friends moved on. "Hello, Mayxaano, good afternoon to you too," he said.

She laughed as she picked up the pace to catch up with him. "Good morning, Ayaanle. I mean, good afternoon."

Ayaanle looked upon Mayxaano approaching with her well-measured strides. Flaunting half-a-dozen books on her right shoulder, she let her left hand dangle at her side. Her crafted hips, a mapped-out middle, and a dark-dipped Afro accentuated the iron-starched blue pants and light amber shirt that she was wearing. He marveled at her beauty and wondered why all the men fawning about her failed to propose marriage. As she got closer, he was arrested by her smile, revealing a set of milk-white teeth all artfully aligned.

"I was thinking," Mayxaano said.

"Thinking about what?" Ayaanle asked.

"Well," she said, by now walking beside him, "I have been cognizant of your ability to recite Somali poetry, specifically what our generation calls songs . . . but I call it poetry, molded in melody. I am also captivated by that mellifluously magnificent voice of yours."

"Hold it, hold it, Mayxaano," Ayaanle said.

"Let me finish, please," Mayxaano begged.

"Well, be my guest then," Ayaanle said.

"If you think that I am going to tell you to devote your entire life to it, you are wrong."

"What do you have in mind then?" Ayaanle asked.

She held her books against her chest. "I would like you to collect a select group of songs and I will do the same—so that we can, first of all, preserve them, and second, write a book about them."

"A book, a book, Mayxaano," shouted Ayaanle.

"Relax, Ayaanle, and just listen to me. What on earth do you think writing a book is about?" Mayxaano asked.

"I have no idea what writing a book is about but I have to tell you, it sounds like an enormous undertaking, and, your Highness, may I remind you of my age if you have not already noticed—I am barely out of short pants."

"Come on," said Mayxaano, holding the books on her hip and placing a hand on his shoulder. "That is why it sounds so ominous, Brother Ayaanle. Listen to me, and please, no interruptions."

"OK, OK. I will not interrupt but . . ."

"No, Ayaanle, no. There are no buts."

"Well, thanks for making it clear that I do not have to think for myself. I don't have a choice anyway, do I?"

"No, you don't. But you have to pay attention to me, Ayaanle, regardless."

He cherished their friendship, with its long history, so he gave in graciously. "All right, Mayxaano. I am all yours."

"The only time that Somali men are romantic is when they are hiding behind the veil of poetry." She hesitated. "We revere it, enjoy it, and most of all fear it but all at once. As you know, poetry in Somalia can spur conflicts that last decades—or bring a prevailing peace. That is why those who love it commit it to memory and pass it on for posterity."

"Mayxaano, you are running away with the topic . . ." interjected Ayaanle.

"You said you were not going to interrupt, Ayaanle," said Mayxaano, drawing her hand away from his shoulder and looking straight at him while they continued walking.

"Sorry, Mayxaano."

". . . because the poetry has a bit of everything that identifies us as Somalis: the tribal bravado, the potential wisdom, the provocative bragging rights . . . as well as a classical paradox between peace and bellicosity. In other words, Ayaanle, it is a treasure. We have just been through the most productive time in terms of theatrical poetry. I mean, songs have come out at an unprecedented rate for the last few years and I dare to predict it will go on with the same pace as we are about to bid the 1970s farewell and usher in the 80's. And I have to say that these songs are very powerful. But you are right. I am digressing and my thoughts are running away with excitement. I have to try to tether myself."

"Thank God. It's about time," said Ayaanle.

"Ayaanle, you gave me your word that you would not do that, remember?" Mayxaano winked.

"Yes, yes, Mayxaano, I'm sorry. I forgot."

"And I'm sorry that I go on and on, but I just love this topic."

"So I noticed," Ayaanle said.

"Anyway," Mayxaano went on. "Let's get back to my reason for seeking you out. I have asked you to help me by collecting a very specific style of songs. These are songs that subdue, serenade, and sedate women. As your mentor, I am recommending that you begin your search with Cumar Dhuule. His songs are the opium of love and life. If I am listening to a tape of his songs, I feel pity for women around the world, wrapped up in romance novels without Dhuule's hypnotic, healing voice, and the alliteration of his aligned stanzas. My God, how I would love for the world to have a taste of the romantic poetry in the Somali language!"

"So, Mayxaano, are you saying that it isn't only Cumar Dhuule, but we Somalis who are naturally gifted when it comes to poetry?"

Mayxaano was already waltzing.

"I am not a pronounced presence at your side
Oh merciless one, I should sever my attachment with you.
Haddaanan ku cuslayn dhankaaga cidla ah
Ciirsilay ana kaa calool go'ay."

Ayaanle thought that he knew Mayxaano well. But now he was stunned to hear her sing and awestruck by the beauty of her rendition of Cumar Dhuule's bass—the clarity of her tempo, the cadence of her delivery. Agape, he stood staring. Never in his life had he heard such a pleasant, female imitation of the legendary Somali singer and lyrist Dhuule.

"And to answer your question, Ayaanle, yes, we Somalis are naturally gifted poets. However, there is no one, no one like him, whose romantic poetry can command your attention with the same intensity of joy. Now, what I am hoping to do is gather songs composed to woo, compliment, and cultivate love. If you pay attention particularly to those songs we call *Darandoori* where a male and female each sings a verse, you would be mesmerized. As you know, there is also another group called *Subcis*, where a man or a woman leads but a choir follows with a harmonious chant. I have to tell you, this is some of the most gratifying, gut wrenching group of literary treasures that I have known. I wish I could share them with the rest of the world, but first we have to introduce them here in our own society. Oh you see, it's now quite clear what I want to mentor you on, and it's crystallizing before me the more I talk it over with you. All you have to do is listen to a bunch of *Darandoori* and *Subcis* songs, select a few of those you deem to be the best, and we will then compare them with the poetic songs of Cumar Dhuule, to see who indeed is the best. We may write together, but more importantly, we will gather memorable material for future generations."

Again, Mayxaano picked up Cumar Dhuule's melodic syrup where she left off:

"Coming to know someone can be lethal
Or a potent blessing and peace
Cakuyeey barashada mid baa cuduroo
Midbaa codcod iyo caano iyo nabad oo."

Ayaanle was dazed. The pleasure of hearing Mayxaano sing left him with a tingling sensation throughout his body. He halted his pace and stared at the tip of a mountain where the horizon met a patch of sun-bathed trees. For the first time in his life, tears gathered in his eyes, a lump grew in his throat, and waves of affection tore at his heart. Yet he did not want her to see him cry. Crying was for women and weak men! And there was no exception to this patriarchal rule, nurtured through the passage of time in the Horn of Africa.

Mayxaano, lost in thought, moved on ahead. "You see, if I give you an example of our *Darandoori* romantic songs, I am 100 percent certain you will join me…" She stopped.

"Ayaanle, where are you?" She turned back to look and saw that Ayaanle was 20 feet behind. "Ayaanle, have I been pouring water into the ocean, or have you been listening to me?"

Now somewhat composed, but still reeling from the shock, Ayaanle caught up with her. "Mayxaano, who are you?"

Though he had tried to mask his emotions with a façade of masculinity, Mayxaano peeled the top layer off. "Ayaanle, I can't believe I got through to you! Did you really cry because I was that bad or was I that good? Well, either way, I feel honored by your emotion. I did not know this soft side of you. I really didn't."

"Well, I thought that I knew you too, Mayxaano. But, but then . . . I think the angels will soon be filing requests for your music."

"Hey, hey, don't chase me away from this world. It's too much fun to be alive. Whenever the time comes that I hear angels filing requests for entertainment, I will know I am dead."

"Ooh, so you have known all along that you are too good for a human audience?" Ayaanle said.

"My younger brother, let us get back to the topic before you blunder yourself into a river of blasphemy."

"No, Mayxaano, I want to know how long you have known that you possessed another gift to share besides math and poetry."

"Sweetie, to be frank with you, I have always known that I could sing, but for a million reasons, it remained hidden behind a cloud of doubt until today when my voice unexpectedly burst through," said Mayxaano. "So lo and behold, you have a front row seat. Now can we please get back to what has been gnawing at me for decades?"

"Of course, your Royalty." Ayaanle extended both hands and opened them up as though he was about to frog leap, like a ballet dancer, dispelling the notion of emotional frailty.

"Did I present my case well?" she asked, playing along.

"Well, your Honor . . ."

"Hold on, hold on. I haven't finished," she interrupted. "Not yet."

"OK, OK, you have the floor."

"Get you. I was trying to see whether you had been paying attention, and come to think of it, I have no complaints. At least not now."

"So would I surmise from that conclusion that I can indulge myself with a rebuttal, a counter-argument, if you will?" Ayaanle asked.

"Wait a minute! Whatever led you to believe that there is a counter-argument? My proposal is dictatorial in nature. The only leniency is that you can take it or leave it. And let me tell you, you are not at liberty to bring up your rude, unrefined, counter offense!"

"Seriously, Mayxaano, I think you are on to something but you have yet to get to the example or examples of *Darandoori* or to the *Subcis* songs you have been clamoring about. Are you aware of that?"

"You are absolutely correct, my sagacious Brother. May I take it as a compliment that all the history that I am pouring on you is paying off?" Mayxaano said.

"For the sake of your vanity, I say 'amen' to that. So let us hear a luxurious note or two from a legend in the making." Ayaanle prompted imaginary applause from an imaginary audience by clapping his hands and bowing.

"Well, *Darandoori*. Which one should I pick?" she asked.

"Here we go again," said Ayaanle. "How on earth would you expect me to know? I am not in . . ."

"Hold it, hold it, it's coming to me, one of my favorites, Salaad Derbi and Saynab Cige. Please listen to this *Darandoori*."

Search deeper for the cause of your distress
And don't cover it in a deer's hide.

Hoos u dhaadhac waxaad hiban
Garag cowl ha saarine.

Ayaanle froze again, every muscle locked. His larynx refused to vibrate and his lips quivered uncontrollably. He stood staring. In his mind, he had just traveled through thousands of miles in a tunnel of joy, yet his fricative vocalization remained frozen, unable to participate in the singing.

He knew the song well. He had sung along with Saynab Cige and Salaad Derbi over the radio. He had seen them live in concert more than 10 times and he had always been moved by the lyrics and their golden voices.

He tried to join her but could not command the will to utter a note. Now he could no longer disguise his feelings, nor did he try to disown them. Tears, drop by drop, rolled down his cheeks. With a heavy heart, Ayaanle knelt, palm covering his eyes.

Mayxaano stopped singing. She held Ayaanle's chin up with one hand and tried to wipe the tears away.

Ayaanle shifted his weight, turning away from her.

Mayxaano began to stroke his hair. "Ayaanle, is my voice so bad that it causes you such pain?" she teased. "Hey, gather yourself or I will continue my wailing. And I'll have you know that this time, I will hold nothing back."

When she stood up, Ayaanle rose, wiped the tears from his eyes, dusted his pants off, and walked after her.

He was lost in thought. He wondered why he was so deeply touched by Mayxaano's singing. Sure, her voice was hypnotizing; sure, it penetrated his heart and forced it to skip a beat or two, but why?

However, he knew why. In fact, this wasn't the first time that he had heard Mayxaano sing.

Falling a few steps behind again, Ayaanle walked back into his past.

Back when he was a boy, his hometown Ceerigaabo did not have a high school of its own. A great number of people in his neighborhood were proud that Mayxaano was going to a high school in another city on a rare scholarship.

Every summer when she was back, she would collect the neighborhood children to offer lessons in Arabic, English, and arithmetic. He remembered how even the neighborhood women, none of whom could read or write but had husbands abroad who wrote to them, would ask her to read those letters as well as write back. As life dictated then, many a Somali man would travel abroad for employment, working as seamen in Europe and on the Arabian peninsula as cheap laborers. It was said that those who had left home were better off, or so the others thought, for they would come back with pouches of cash to flaunt and paint over the hardship they had endured for every penny.

Ayaanle remembered Mayxaano's last tutoring class. She had sung, then soon after, both she and her family vanished from the city. He had not seen her again until many years later, when he arrived at Sheikh High School for classes.

As a young boy who lived next door to her and had the privilege of extra access to her, compared to the other children she tutored, it was a devastating loss. Yet, the truth was worse when he learned that she was never going to return. He had first heard the news from the neighborhood. When it seemed the loss was too much to bear, he sought solace in his Grandmother.

She held his hands and pulled him towards her, hugged him tight, and sat him in her lap. "My child, you are too young to know all the cruel things that grownups inflict on each other, and by extension on their children," she said. "It is true, Mayxaano and her family have left this town, never to come back."

"But why, Grandma, why?" he pleaded.

"The neighbors caused you this grief," she responded.

Tears flowing his eyes, he asked, "What happened? Did they hurt her, Grandma?"

His grandmother wiped his tears away and said, "No, no, my child. They didn't hurt her physically, no. They didn't."

"Then tell me what, Grandma, tell me. What did they do to her?"

"If I tell you, I want you never to share with anyone, never, ever. And never talk to anybody about her or her family if you want them to live in peace."

"I swear, Grandma, I swear I will never share it with anyone. Just tell me."

"I am told that at the end of Mayxaano's last tutorial class, she sang to the children. Some parents claimed that in doing so, she cast a curse on the children which, if repeated, could cause a great harm because of 'Who-she-is.' So they threatened her life."

Thinking that he was in deep trouble, too, Ayaanle did not tell his grandmother that he was there when Mayxaano had sung to them. As a matter of fact, Mayxaano herself had not known that he was there.

"What do you mean by 'Who-she-is?'" Ayaanle asked.

"My child, you will only understand 'Who-Mayxaano-is' when you grow up. Now, I want you to be a man and stop crying. Don't ever talk about what I shared with you, OK?"

Befuddled and feeling guilty all at once, Ayaanle had thought it best to leave it all alone. Now that he was almost a man, his grandmother's statement, "My child, you will only understand Who-Mayxaano-is when you grow up," was no less confusing than when he was a young boy sworn to secrecy. One thing was quite clear, however: that whatever his grandmother was not willing to say aloud at the time was ominously vile.

But what was it?

All he knew was that simply by singing in such a superior voice Mayxaano fell from grace because of "who she is." Was it because she was from a poor family? No, there were other poor families, too, but none were treated the same as Mayxaano's. Was it because her father was dead? No, no. It was not that either, for there were others whose fathers were no longer alive.

Ayaanle took inventory of how the neighborhood affairs were conducted: how disputes were adjudicated, how weddings and newborn ceremonies were celebrated, and how leaders were selected. He could see a pattern emerging: that Mayxaano and her family were not in any decision-making roles. Did that have anything to do with their clan affiliation?

He realized that both Mayxaano and her mother kept their distance by staying away from neighborhood social gathering sites. He could not account for a single social event they participated in. Goodness grief, the family must have been guarding their secret alone.

It was quite clear to him now that both Mayxaano herself, and Cumar Dhuule, the man whom she was self-sworn to write about, were kin of the same "Midgaan" clan, one of the most ostracized minorities in Somalia. In Mayxaano's case, he could sense that behind her beauty and talent, she had hidden layers of grief and pain. On top of that, she was a woman. Thus, he was reminded why he as her protégé was overcome with emotion. He was shedding her tears for her.

He understood why she had been keeping her voice behind that cloud and was not willing to allow it to ring out in public. And by inadvertently once calling attention to her sensual voice, she was accused of exercising lascivious behavior. By calling it a "curse," his grandmother was sanitizing it so that she could share it with a child.

All those men swarming about her like bees were only trying to have her for dessert. Not a single one of them would have been courageous enough to take her for a wife! In their eyes, she was not worthy of their matrimonial crown. In reality, he thought, they are the ones not worthy of her shoes.

During the next few minutes, they walked side by side, their solemn silence broken only by the sound of their footsteps, determined to press on. As they approached the outskirts of the small town, the footpath they were on diverged and each chose a different route. Both proceeded with a cautious gait.

Mayxaano was turning a corner when waves of music greeted her. She stopped and looked back to see whether Ayaanle had heard the same melodic voice that would have caused world dignitaries to beg for more.

Ayaanle, too, had heard the lilting notes of Subcis coming from two or three blocks away, on the other side of the small town. "Mayxaano, do you hear that?" he shouted.

"Yes, I do, but who is it?" Mayxaano shouted back.

"Who cares who, it's beautiful. Let's go and see."

In earnest, they moved to where the blissful melody was originating. The closer they got, the calmer and the more soothingly captivating the harmony became. Soon they encountered a half-dozen or so boys and girls behind an abandoned building, under the shade of a huge eucalyptus tree, singing the mesmerizing tune.

There is a thorn in the sole of my foot
Of which I cannot escape the pain…
Ragaadeyoo roori karmaayee
Ribateye yaa dhankale ka rogoo

First, they thought there was one lead singer with a golden voice, but then they realized that each student would take a line of Cumar Dhuule's "Dance with Me, Dhudi." It would reach a crescendo and, in chorus, the students would follow with another verse. The chorus would end, and then another solo would erupt in a cascading croon that could calm a seething king. The accompanying musical instruments were as simple as a lute and a drum. Yet the joy of this concert was a thousand-fold, giving reason to Mayxaano's plea to collect Cumar Dhuule's treasures.

As the impromptu corner concert came to an end, Ayaanle realized that the most venerated Sheikh of the small town was in the audience. It was this Sheikh that Ayaanle had heard vociferously preach against music of any kind. It dawned on him then that the entire population of the small town was present. Even the slothful, lazy minded Cambaro-shaal, who had never been seen civilly seated, was now sitting in an armchair, totally absorbed, keeping her only goat beside her by holding tightly to its ear. So when people began to disperse, Ayaanle turned to Mayxaano. "Mayxaano," he said, "you just got yourself an apprentice, but I hope the market will be big enough for both of us."

She walked away, laughing. At about a 30-yard distance, she looked back. Ayaanle was still standing where she left him.

"Ayaanle," he heard her cry out, "he who waits for inspiration only harvests the pain begotten by time wasted. . . . So Cumar Dhuule is your choice, I gather. Don't leave me hanging!" She turned on her heels and moved off.

So Mayxaano had decided to face Somali social demons head on. Ayaanle wondered how much help he was going to be to her and how.

The Mayxaano Chronicles:
A Whip of Words

It was 11 o'clock in the morning and the omnipresent East African sun stood sentinel, not simply staring but also guiding its gamma rays onto God's land. The stores serving the splendid city of Burco—the epicenter of Somalia, a city all roads anywhere in the country eventually converged on—bellowed, pregnant with people. A pure blue sky, purged of pollution, put on a perfect smile.

That morning the weather had quickly warmed into the 70s, then edged on to the 80s, and now just rested there. The bustling public was not aware of what Mother Nature had in store for them later in the day. And why would they be? It was blissfully pleasant and the people of Burco were just milling about on the streets.

The eastbound station teemed with trucks, pulsing with parties of all ages haggling for the lowest fare. Among them were those who pestered passengers for *safar salaama* blessing—one of a thousand ways that sullen souls would have the passengers believe that by giving alms, they could pay for benediction to save themselves from "God's boiling wrath." So the passengers would pay them off.

Mayxaano walked through the crowd, feasting on a visual tour of a perfect, tranquil day. At that moment, though, what was weighing on her mind was what the mood of a city feels like early in the morning before most people are out and about. More than any other urban habitat that she knew, Burco uniquely conveyed its message about life with the motorcycles' cruising roar in the west echoing off the street walls; the occasional, rhythmic revving of trucks; and the marvelous music created by Burco's cooing pigeons, out of sync with the hum of human voices yet magical in its own way.

Nothing was out of the ordinary. The weather was dry but not too dry; warm but not too warm; and passive but not so passive that it would burden you with boredom.

Mayxaano, on her spring recess from teaching, took a notebook and pen from her purse. Yet she did not write a thing. She walked past the Shell gas station, buzzing with eastbound trucks. Savoring a victory that a soccer team from Ceerigaabo had secured the day before against a much-too-favored team from Hargeisa, she was joyous and still cheering on Dalmar, the unsung hero of the team. She marveled how he masterfully maneuvered the ball between much older men and delivered the unpredicted and unprecedented win. She swore to herself that she was the first one who had taught Dalmar his ABCs. So mature and now he carried the whole team on his back.

A few yards away, she entered the Daalo restaurant, corralled within a wire fence. The perimeter around it was populated by acacia trees that stood shoulder to shoulder, casting shadows shared beneath them. In each shadow, two or more tables and chairs were furnished for leisure time.

It would not take a full minute to have a waiter with a tray come to you, whimpering, "What are you going to order?" In a second you would hear him pelting away, "*Waar sagaal laydha ah keen, waar sagaal laydha ah keen, waar sagaal laydha ah keen* [Nine cups of tea outside, nine cups of tea outside, nine cups of tea outside]." No one ever bothered to ask the waiter what the difference was between nine cups of tea outside and nine cups of tea inside? Were they cooked at different temperatures? Were the outside patrons more or less valued than the inside ones? It was—and still is even today—the same for the waiters as well. Upon reaching the tables, they ask the same question, year in and year out: "What are you going to order?" And the patrons always have the banality to respond, "Bring me a cup of tea with milk!" It was no secret that the offerings were limited, but the waiters still hoped that they would come up with a creative way or two to order from the same. Yet customers always failed them by responding with the ready-made mantra of "Bring me a cup of tea." The only choices were, "Bring me a cup of tea with milk" or "Bring me a cup of tea without." There had been rare occasions, however, when one patron would feel fancy and artful and order the waiter with the word "listen." Mind you, people never use the word "please" in this part of the world, particularly in Burco. "Listen, bring me a cup of tea that is short."

Once, customers heard a man of means shouting to a waiter, "Hey, hey, listen up, Man, add some more milk on mine, OK? And one more thing, let it be hot; the last time I was here a year ago, I poured the whole damn cup on the ground. It was too damn cool."

"It wasn't me, you fool," the waiter fended off.

"I don't care who it was. It was this tea shop anyway," the man shouted back.

The residents of Burco would like to believe that this place, Daalo, was a bit different from other restaurants or teashops. For one, it was the premier eatery in Burco, and second, you could order both tea and a variety of food dishes that were so well known that you wouldn't need to ask for a menu. As a matter of fact, there was no menu even if you had wanted to see one. Let it be known though that a diner could not always count on food dishes being available as well affordable. But customers could always count on a cup of tea with or without milk and afford it as well!

Mayxaano took one of the unoccupied tables, seated herself, and arranged her notebook and pen on the table. She had opened the pages and begun to write furiously when a waiter showed up and asked, "What are you going to order?" Not, "What would you like to order?" Or, "May I take your order, please?"

"May I have a cup of tea?" Mayxaano asked, breaking a million years of monotonous rudeness by simply saying the two words "May I," implying that she wanted a cup of tea "with milk." When she spoke, she neither looked away from her writing nor lifted her pen.

The waiter moved on to the next table, collecting empty cups from a boisterous group of high school boys with distinctive Afro hair styles. As he stacked the empty cups on the tray, he sang aloud how much money the boys had to pay. "*Waa saddex shillin iyo badh, waa saddax shillin iyo badh, waa saddax shillin iyo badh* [three shillings and a half, three shillings and a half, three shillings and a half...]!"

"Heeeey," one of them interrupted. "Camel-boy, stop that. You aren't watering camels or cows or whatever it was that you used to raise as a nomad. You can't sing to us as though we're livestock."

"Let your mother know that, not me," the waiter responded in a self-assured tone.

"Ooooh, are you going to stay seated while this fellow drags your mother into this?" one of the boys shouted to his friend.

"Oooh, maybe you're not man enough to defend her honor!" chided another.

Before he finished the sentence, the insulted boy was on his feet, rolling up his sleeves. He jumped on the waiter, grabbed him by the collar of his shirt, and said, "Take that back, you bastard! Take that back, I said!"

The waiter, who looked to be the weaker of the two, calmly placed the tray on the table. He grabbed the boy by the wrist, wrenching the now contorted hand behind his back.

"You seem to be man enough to taunt," he roared, twisting the hand tighter, "but not man enough to hold your ground, you Bastard Schoolboy. Look, I can say what I want about your mother now, because you aren't man enough to stand up for her."

"Ouch, ouch, ooooouuuuuuuuuuuuuch, let me go," screamed the schoolboy, while the rest of his friends laughed, watching. "Let me go."

"Hey, come on, you idiot. You going to let that Camel-boy humiliate you like that?" shouted one.

The waiter, whose clothing had given him away as a nomad, looked furious. Calling him a Camel-boy was implying that he was dumb, illiterate, untamed or all three. He seemed unwilling to take that kind of torment from boys who had been fortunate enough to have someone pay for their schooling. So as soon as he heard another boy call him Camel-boy, he let go of the first one and lunged at the other. The schoolboy tried to teach the waiter a lesson by greeting him with a punch, aiming right at his nose. But the agile waiter dodged, pasted himself onto the lower end of the schoolboy, and, within a second, swirled him about, letting him loose. Then, as he began falling, the waiter tripped him with his right leg. The schoolboy fell hard to the ground, face first. His cheek smacked against the dirt, his shoulder dived into the sandy earth, and he choked on a mouthful of sand and dust. The gawkers around them, mostly men, stood up and clapped their hands, laughing. Now the first schoolboy, who had lost his initial attempt to intimidate the waiter, took his shirt off and puffed up his chest before raising his fists, if for no other reason than to show off. Yet when the waiter gave him the let-us-get-on-with-it wave, the schoolboy took one step back. Every time the waiter took one step forward, the schoolboy took two back until he stumbled backwards over his friend who was still struggling to regain his feet.

Laughter, now louder, lacerated the lazy air as Mayxaano stood up and walked over to the waiter. Gently, but with authority, she took his hand, prying him apart from the boys, and said, "Enough, enough already," in her most commanding teacher's voice.

"You guys, shame on you," she bellowed to a bunch of men at a nearby table. "How dare you watch these boys beat up one another like the wild-wild-west? Is this a movie?"

Embarrassed by the whip of words Mayxaano had let loose, a dozen or so men moved to help the boys by lifting them to their feet, dusting them off, and counseling them to calm down. Suddenly the other two friends, who had been watching, now chose to join the fight. From behind the wall of adult men, they timidly shouted, "Camel-boy. Camel-boy. Come and get this, come and get this."

Mayxaano pulled the waiter away from the crowd. "Listen, whatever they say to you, don't show it's gotten to you. OK?"

"I can't bear it," the waiter said, tears dripping down his cheeks. "These bastards think they're better than me because they go to school. I would love to swap places with them for a day. I would have loved to go to school but I never had the opportunity when I was a boy."

"You're still a young boy to me," said Mayxaano.

"Yes, but I have to work as a man. My father died not long ago and my mother has seven children to care for. So it is my duty to help raise them. And every damn day, these assholes from rich families come here and give me grief."

The manager came out of the restaurant. "Hey, Boy, what the hell are you…" But before he finished his sentence, he saw Mayxaano holding his waiter's hand, consoling him.

"He had a bit of a rowdy crowd," Mayxaano volunteered as the manager began to approach.

"Don't tell me that he had a fight again. Didn't I tell you no more fighting or else I would let you go?"

"Hold it, hold it, sir, it was not his fault."

"Yes, I know, I know. The last one wasn't his fault either, and the one before that wasn't and the one before and the other… You see what I mean," the manager babbled on.

"Yes, maybe so in your eyes but…"

"Maybe so in my eyes, you are exac…." The manager stopped, interrupting himself. "Hey! Don't I know you from somewhere?"

"Well, I don't know, do you?" She let go of the waiter.

"Go and get those empty tea glasses off that table and take the orders from those tables," he told the waiter, showing no further sign of anger. "Let me see, you have a unique name if I can remember; let me see if I can recall. Mayxaaaaaaaaano, Mayxaano, right?"

"Yes, that is me…"

"Is that still your name?"

"Yes, it is. I take it that you don't like it?"

"No, no, as a matter fact, I love it. What an unusual name."

"I prefer the first adjective you used, 'unique.'"

"Unique it is. What does it mean and who named you anyway?"

"Well," Mayxaano began, "as to the former question, I have no idea what it means and I don't care. I love my name! And to the latter, it was my mother's cousin Qoran, God rest her soul, who named me." She paused. "But I have to tell you that I am quite embarrassed that I do not have the slightest idea who you are and how you know me or from where."

"Have you anything to fear?" the manager asked.

"Please. Not the least, sir. I haven't been lucky enough to have multiple suitors nor have I had a husband who would cause me to weep."

"I see. You were so young when I last saw you. But if I tell you who I am, I am quite certain you will remember me and a lot more!"

As Mayxaano looked at him carefully, something triggered her memory. Was it the tiny gap between his front teeth? Was it the now barely visible scar above his left eyebrow that had almost faded away with time? Was it the minute dot on the side of his iris? She couldn't tell which, but her childhood memory broke the gate with might.

"I cannot believe it," she screamed. "Xariir, is it you?"

"Yes, Mayxaano, it is me."

"You have completely changed." She stood up and thrust her right hand forward to shake his, as the culture dictated. In Somalia in those days, shaking the hands of the opposite sex was the common greeting. The two exchanged warm pleasantries by shaking hands but averted each other's eyes as the custom dictated, too.

"I can't believe my eyes, Mayxaano. You are as beautiful as ever," he said.

"Don't flatter me. I am too old for that today, but it worked miracles on me when I was young, and every time you and your cousin, Bilaal, poured…" She stopped, and gently pulled her hand away.

"It is as true today as it was then," he responded, not

noticing that Mayxaano was close to tears as she uttered the name Bilaal.

Mayxaano turned to hide her emotions. "Oh, let me gather my books, please."

"Hey, Mayxaano, don't leave. I'm going to get off soon, in a half hour or so. Please wait for me. We have a lot to catch up with. Please, stay seated," he added.

"Did he say please? He must not have been in northern Somalia too long, particularly not in Burco," she said to herself, too soft for him to hear. But then she was overwhelmed by emotions that she was not willing to share today. *Not so fast*, she told herself.

"Mayxaano, please order some food and I'll be right back," said Xariir, as he took off back into the restaurant.

Mayxaano picked up her notebook, patted it, and put the pen on it as though she were about to hand both over to an eager student.

During the next half hour, they each plunged into the memory of a past they had shared. For Mayxaano, it was the memory of her first and last meaningful crush, and for Xariir, it was the memory of their shared history. Twelve years earlier, during the mid-1960s, Bilaal, Xariir's cousin, and Xariir himself noticed a blossoming flower paying visits to their beautiful next door neighbor, Abyan. Abyan displayed disinterest and a dampened spirit toward the two not-so-daring teens who enviously watched the girls' encounters at the adjacent door. Because of their age and shyness, both boys had not dared to approach the majestic creature called Mayxaano until she met them half way. The first few times she had arrived at the house, Mayxaano waved at the boys, peeking out from the neighboring door. As their bravery heightened, they began waiting on the doorstep for her departure. They were infatuated with both women and would often fantasize aloud about being invited into the house. But usually Abyan would open the door and stick just her head out or extend one long slender arm to wave goodbye to her friend. Mayxaano, however, would tempt the boys even further by actually waving goodbye directly at them as well. The boys later learned that Abyan had referred to them as "the villains."

"Hey, she said 'Hello, how are you?' to me," one of the boys would yell to the other every time Mayxaano waved at them.

"Well, you're mistaken, because if you were paying attention, you would have been able to see that she was looking at me," the other would counter.

"How on earth would you know who she was looking at from 40 feet away?" the first would respond.

This went on and on unabated until finally Xariir had the gall to challenge the girl's taste in poetry. Not just poems, but the newest genre called songs, normally rationed out by radio Mogadishu or Hargeisa.

Sitting at the restaurant table, Mayxaano was flooded with memories of two nervous, giggling boys—almost men—sitting on the front stoop of their house when she would visit their neighbor and her best friend, Abyan.

From the first day she saw the boys, who were about two to three years older than she and Abyan, they had shown a bit of mystique about them and she liked them both. They were polite, much too polite for schoolboys of their age from the area; they were shy but not too shy to be shackled by it; and they were attentive but not too attentive to be overbearing. When Mayxaano had begun inquiring about their background, Abyan initially advised her not to bother, but Mayxaano had persisted until Abyan told her that the boys were cousins who had been born in a part of the British colonial empire known as

Aden, Yemen. When they were very young they had moved to Nairobi, Kenya but after Somalia's independence, their families returned to Somalia and settled in Mogadishu. Xariir's maternal uncle, Bilaal's father, was one of the first Somali cabinet ministers of the new government. She recalled that the boys had come to the city of Ceerigaabo, where their parents had originated in Somalia, to spend their summer vacation with relatives.

As the flood of memories rushed through her, feelings from the past also emerged. She felt how, at the beginning, she liked to see the two cousins from a distance, then how she enjoyed waving at them, then how she wanted to hear them say hello, and in the end, how she wanted to recite poetry with them but, most importantly, how she soon fell for one of them.

"What are you going to order? Hello."

"Hah," Mayxaano looked up, realizing that another waiter, not the same one who had the fight a few minutes ago, was standing over her.

Did he hear me talking to myself? How long has he been here? Oh, he probably thinks I am a lunatic by now, she thought.

"Lady, are you going to order something or what?" the waiter snorted.

She had been staring at him. "Oh, my God," she said, but then caught herself. "Wait a minute, Boy, why don't you have some gentlemanly manners and first tell me what you have to offer for choice here. Let's start from there."

"Well, it is the same as we had yesterday and the day before and the day before and on and on, do you get it? Now, do you want to order something or what?"

Mayxaano laughed. She laughed because the waiter was serious and she laughed at the absurdity of his logic and the irony involved. Finally he was about to move on, wearing his contempt on his face, when Xariir came back and took a seat next to her.

"Hello, what did I miss?" Xariir asked

"Or what are you interrupting?" Mayxaano added, winking.

"Well, well, well. Should I leave the two of you alone?" asked Xariir, winking back at Mayxaano.

Absolutely unfazed by the presence of his boss, the waiter joined in, "This lady has taken so much time that I could have fed a village! I have been here since, oh, when you sent me this morning, and she has not yet ordered!"

"But Mataan, that was yesterday, wasn't it? I am just kidding," said Xariir.

Xariir stood up, patted the waiter on the shoulder, pulled him aside and whispered, "I don't believe that you could have fed a fly with those minutes, let alone fed a village. You are a great waiter and we all know that, but 10 to 20 seconds or so? Come on, Mataan?"

The waiter laughed, relaxed, apologized to Mayxaano and moved on to the next table.

"That is Burco for you, isn't it?" stated Mayxaano with a sarcastic touch. "What did you tell him?"

"Well, you will not believe it but…?"

"But what?"

"I told him that he might have scared off a potential marriage prospect!" responded Xariir. However, the minute the word "marriage" passed his lips, Xariir appeared to regret saying it.

"My God, you are not that much different except that you have been assimilated and now speak Burco's language," Mayxaano said.

"'When in Rome' and you know the rest…."

"It is you that I am mad at now," said Mayxaano. "We have

not seen each other for close to two decades and look at the first thing you did! You pulled Burco on me, and worse, you sided with your discourteous waiter. Why would that surprise me? I know Somali men and you are all the same, plus Burco!"

"I would have preferred to see the innocent, polite teenager of 1960 in Ceerigaabo again," she added.

"And how are you too? You know, you have not changed a bit. You still seem to have the same assailing wit and savvy soul about you. Not backing down an inch nor sacrificing a second."

"I am sorry, Xariir, but I am curious; what on earth did you say to him that subdued him so fast?"

"Well, I told him that you work for the NSS." He cringed again as he realized that this was a poor joke as well. Maybe Mayxaano did work for the notorious, oppressive National Security Service unit.

"Why didn't I think of that? Obviously that would shut anybody up. Poor guy," Mayxaano said.

"Well, I actually told him that you are the Queen of Nice and that you deserve better from him. What else would I be able to say about you after so long a time?" said Xariir.

"Nothing else, I guess, and you should be nice to me after all these years," said Mayxaano.

"Wow, Mayxaano, tell me about yourself, fast, or I'm going to die on this operating table," said Xariir.

"There isn't much to tell. I grew up fast, chose to teach, and stayed single, lest I produce undesirable progenies nobody wants to be around, like you and your insolent waiter."

"You don't say. I don't blame you, but where do you teach and what?"

"I am teaching Math as well as a Somali Language Literature course at Sheikh Secondary School," Mayxaano said.

"What an odd combination, how did that come about and why?" Xariir asked.

"Well, where do I start...?"

"Wait. Hold on, hold on. Have you ordered anything to eat yet?"

"No. Didn't you just chase my insolent waiter away?"

"I'll be right back." Xariir jumped up and was about to run into the kitchen when Mayxaano interrupted.

"Wait, wait. What are you going to get for me? You know it isn't lunch time yet, and we are way past breakfast."

"Come on, Mayxaano, this is not New York, Paris, or London, wherever it was that you went to college. Here we don't have big menus with lots to choose from." Xariir put both hands on the edge of the table and pressed his weight on his elbows.

"How do you know that I even went to college? I am not from a fancy family, you know," Mayxaano quipped. She put her hand on his arm, staring at him in defiance of the cultural dictum.

"Mayxaano, I know you went to college abroad. That much I know about you." Xariir briefly touched the top of her arm before gently pulling away with a slight laugh. He turned around and walked briskly back to the kitchen.

Mayxaano looked around her, tentative, and saw that within the enclosure, under the shade of the acacia trees, those well-polished, unpainted tables and chairs were populated with the people of Burco, both male and female, drinking tea, laughing and chatting. Every minute, more diners would arrive while others left. She smelled the fresh air and the earth beneath her, dampened and cooled by water that had been sprinkled on it, emitting an aura of impending rain.

Suddenly the cries of the 'Camel-boy' waiter, "*Waar sigaal*

laydha ah keen, waar sagaal laydha ah keen," assaulted her hearing again. She looked up and saw that not a single emotional scar remained from his earlier sparring.

Why is he still shouting "Nine cups of tea outside?" Mayxaano asked herself. *He was saying nine when I arrived, right? I might not have heard him right the first time around.*

"Here we go," Xariir interrupted her. He brought a tray with three plates on it, put one on the table, and took a glass of tea out of the hands of another waiter. The waiter took the tray away and went back to the kitchen. Mayxaano looked down at a delectable dish of mutton stew with curry, hot peppers, onion and tomatoes.

"Wow, this looks good and smells great, too," Mayxaano said. She walked to a water tap in a corner of the restaurant's front door to wash her hands. She returned, seated herself, looked at the two different breads on the table, hesitated, then picked the spongy, flat one and began to eat.

"So Mayxaano, how on earth did you manage to branch out into two unrelated fields and particularly fields of study that are out of the norm for Somali females?" Xariir did not hide his admiration. What he did not say aloud but was alluding to was that men had claimed exclusive ownership of Somali poetry, although throughout history women had played a pivotal role by actually composing it. And around the globe, not just in Somalia, few women sought out Math as a course of study and even less as a profession.

"Well, actually, both subjects chose me," Mayxaano said, holding her lips tight while she swallowed a portion of the mutton stew.

"I knew that you had so much passion for Somali poetry but I thought it was going to fade away with adolescence."

"It never did. As a matter of fact, I have to tell you that you guys both had a hand in that..."

"Both who, Mayxaano?" Xariir interrupted.

"Both you and—and—and—Bilaal," she said, the words halting.

"How is that?"

"Remember that you used to come to us with a fresh song or poem every day during your summer vacation?" Mayxaano took another bite of the mutton stew and bread.

Xariir laughed so hard that he almost fell off his chair.

Mayxaano swallowed, tried to wipe the food off her mouth, and, realizing that she did not have a hand towel, looked at him.

"I'm sorry," Xariir said and started waving to the waiter.

"*Toban laydha ah, toban laydha ah:* 10 cups of tea outside, 10 cups of tea outside," the waiter chanted as he approached.

"Can you get us a hand-towel?" Xariir blurted.

"*Waar toban laydha ah, toban laydha,*" continued the waiter as he pulled up a towel from a pile draped over his shoulder and handed it to Xariir.

"He is one of the best, but has a real bad temper that we haven't been able to tame. He fights all the time and against anybody and everybody," Xariir volunteered.

"Well, I was going to tell you not to fire him, because you were rough on him earlier."

"Fire him? I dare not do that. I like the guy. He is very dependable, honest, and hard working. Where I am going to find anybody like him?"

"You were rough on him, I said, did you hear that? And is that how you show your appreciation? There is a lot on his mind. Have you ever sat down with him just to talk?"

"No."

"Do you know him?"

"Do I know him?"

"Xariir, that's what I asked, do you know him?"

"Aw, Mayxaano, you still mother everybody. Do you mean have I ever talked to him about his life and so on? Not really. Maybe I should, hah?"

"Please do. He is a proud young man, and these city boys are picking on him. But he isn't going to let them get away with an inch. And just to let you know, he's burdened by the loss of his father…"

"How do you know?" interrupted Xariir.

"Oh, my God, you men, you never get it, do you? Because I asked." Mayxaano began to eat again.

"OK, OK. You got all that out of him in the two minutes that you were keeping him from harming himself?"

"He wasn't harming himself, he was whipping their asses and may I add with flair as well!"

"I get the message, Mayxaano. I do, I really do. So let's go back to your story now, before the dusk dispatches its demons on us."

"Fire the other insolent, arrogant one, who I think is your cousin," Mayxaano said.

Xariir laughed. "How the hell did you figure that one out?"

"Where was I with my life story anyway?" Mayxaano ignored Xariir's question. "I have to warn you though, my life story is not as hot as your meal."

"Why don't you let me be the judge of that?" Xariir said. "Before you resume, I have to tell you a secret that I have not shared with anyone for almost 15 years."

"Why do you want to share this secret now?" Mayxaano asked.

"Because it doesn't serve any purpose for me to keep it to myself. Besides I can't carry it alone anymore."

"So, are you going to get it over with before 'the dusk

arrives,' just to borrow a word from a wise man?" She winked.

"I'll get to it if the foxy Mayxaano would let me finish?"

"Allright, the 'foxy Mayxaano' is dying to hear the secret."

"Remember you said that we, Bilaal and I, used to bring a song or poem everyday to enjoy?"

"Yes."

"What you didn't know was that once we knew that you were consuming our poetry and songs voraciously, we got drunk with your attention and wanted more. The problem, however, was every time we departed your company, you had consumed all we had to offer. We would immediately scavenge poems for the next week. We sought out everyone: the old, insane, blind, poor and rich, just to have one song or a poem to share with the Queens. We would go around the neighborhood, asking elderly women to recite poems by heart. They knew hundreds! And we would stalk elderly men for the same reason. Thank God, they all graciously shared their poetic repertoires. Boy, that was fun. Thus, neither poets nor poetry were tough to find, because everybody was a poet or poetess then, but songs were more difficult to come by. Remember that sometimes, we didn't show up for days?"

"No, I don't remember that. I only remember that you served us well," Mayxaano said.

"Serve my nose and nape! That was what doomed us. Sometimes we would not get a single song, so we would not dare come back to see you. As a matter of fact, we would not even return to our house. One time, I recall that we slept over at a guy's house that we would have nothing to do with otherwise. He had a radio, you know."

"I thought you had a radio of your own," said Mayxaano.

"You really thought we did?"

"Boy, yes I can recall how rare the radio thing was though.

There were very few in the whole city of Ceerigaabo and we thought yours was one of them!"

"Right! We wanted you to believe that," Xariir elaborated. "Do you also remember that songs were such a new genre that you could only hear them on the radio on very rare occasions?"

"I remember that you could neither hear nor find songs anywhere else," Mayxaano said.

"Right. There were so few radios and even when you could find one, it was only on rare, and I stress the word 'rare,' occasions that a song or songs would be played. Do you remember that?"

"Yes, I do. And to make the matter worse, whatever song was on might not have been the right one," Mayxaano said.

"Wow. You're absolutely right. How painful was that? Oh, old times!" said Xariir. "So anyway," he continued, "this became an expensive, exhausting habit. We had to keep up the supply. Those damn songs that you used to dance to and that made you shiver with ecstasy every time we recited the first verse put us in trouble to the point where we could have been taken to jail!"

"Now you are exaggerating, Xariir," Mayxaano said, laughing.

"No, Mayxaano, I wish I were."

"How so?"

"Well, remember that radio we used to listen to sometimes?" asked Xariir.

"Yes."

"Did you know how we got it in the first place and what eventually happened to it?"

"No, I didn't and didn't care."

"You're right, you didn't care but you did care about the

songs. I'm ashamed to tell you that we stole that radio!"

"Whaaaaat?" Mayxaano shouted, pushing her plate away, then covering her mouth with both hands.

"And that's not all, Mayxaano. Every time we ran out of batteries—which seemed every hour or a half-hour—we stole them too. As you recall, they cost a fortune then."

"We thought you were too rich to do dumb things like that..."

"Well, we weren't that rich after all, were we?"

"Hearing this from you now, no."

"Listen to this, please. We wanted you to believe that we were very smart, you see! We would go back to the same shop from where we had stolen the radio and then steal batteries, too. And, wouldn't you know it, we got caught. The shopkeeper interrogated us until we confessed to our crime. He said that he was not going to tell anyone if we not only would leave his shop alone but promise him never to steal from anyone ever again. And bring the radio back, he demanded."

Mayxaano laughed so loud that some people began to stare.

"So, Mayxaano, please keep it to yourself when you say so lightly that it was all fun," Xariir added, and began to laugh, too.

"*Laba iyo toban laydha ah, waar lama iyo toban baa laydha* [12 cups of tea outside]." The waiter was back, clearing Mayxaano and Xariir's table. As he collected the dirty dishes onto his tray, he kept chanting, "*Laba iyo toban laydha ah* [12 cups of tea outside.]" Once more, Mayxaano, who was now a bit more composed but still laughing, was wondering why the waiter would enjoy saying, "This many cups of tea outside," rather than simply "I need four, five, ten" or whatever the count was, just omitting "outside" or "inside"?

"Are we ever going to get to your story?" Xariir asked.

"I didn't know that I had such an effect on men. My God,

that feels great," Mayxaano said, and started laughing again. "But you have to finish yours first, then ask about mine, maybe both the present and past," she added.

"Why do I have the feeling that you aren't going to be sympathetic to our past misery?"

"Because it is not my fault that I didn't know until now about the criminal enterprise, carried out under the intent of gaining our attention but with cursed stupidity," said Mayxaano.

"What can I tell you? We lived up to the motto of 'love makes you do stupid things.' Whoever said that was a wise man," said Xariir.

"That wasn't love; and the only part of the statement that's true is the stupidity part."

"Mayxaano, you were the patron of the total prize, stupidity or not. So please, don't pretend that you had no part to play in this."

"Maybe so, but I think Abyan and I were at least smart enough to know that had you been arrested, we would have assumed no responsibility for your actions. Remember we were staying home and you were stealing!"

"I know that now, but then we were feeding 'your voracious appetite for poetry,'" said Xariir. "And anyone who knows anything about being a teenager would have understood it. Definitely a court would not have missed the reason why we were so devoted and daringly loyal. But Mayxaano, do you know what the tune of the misfortune was?"

"Please, repeat that, what did you say, the tune of the misfortune? I've never heard that before."

"The bastard shop owner called us a month later, indicting us. He was the judge, jury and prosecutor. But the fact that we were guilty helped him mount a good case against us."

Abruptly, his demeanor changed as he looked on at her.

He sensed that whatever was left to tell could be too painful and bothersome. In seconds, the glowing smile vanished. His eyes glazed over and his humor dimmed. Looking at Mayxaano, he saw that her excitement had suddenly ebbed as well. Seconds ticked by before Xariir tried to steer the conversation back to catching up with each other's past and present.

It was at that moment that Xariir realized they had arrived at the gate guarding a past that they both wanted to keep at bay. What he could not guess was whether Mayxaano was going to be able to tell him about all that had transpired during the decade or so they had been apart.

"So Mayxaano, you still haven't told me how you landed a job simultaneously teaching Somali literature and Math?" Xariir asked.

"There isn't much to tell," Mayxaano began. "I can simply say I went to college, alas, not where you fancied it to be, but in Mogadishu. I loved them both, so I majored in them and am now teaching both, despite men's initial disbelief and demeaning manner. Those tend to disappear once I display my prowess in both. What was fortuitous was how I have grown to love them both. You see, at first I was not attached to either of the two, and what you have chosen not to remember was how you and, and, and…" She hesitated, her voice hoarse. She stood, moved to the fence, and stared at the blue sky. It was obvious that the years had not erased the pain attached to the name she was having a hard time saying.

Xariir leaned on the fence next to her. Looking at the same imaginary stage in the distance, he sensed that Mayxaano could no longer contain herself. She was crying. And he could not do a thing. He could not get close to comfort or console her. He could only curse, hoping to cool himself off. The pain carried by both, but particularly by Mayxaano, was palpable.

Xariir knew that he was at his weakest moment. How he wanted to reach out and touch Mayxaano, to pull her away from the fence and hold her! But he could not. Social and cultural taboos prevented him. Somewhere in the back of his mind, he could hear the soft but vile voices of the social norm, whispering, "Whatever you might let yourself become entangled with, let not one of them be holding a woman in public that you are neither married nor related to." On rare, extremely rare occasions, when a woman is so distraught over a death in the family or, God forbid, seized by the pain of impending childbirth, there was a tacit yet tepid social tolerance for touching between the sexes. But only if the woman was in such distress that she was on the fringe of tearing her clothes off. And maybe, maybe a man could physically intervene if two women were actually fighting in public.

So now Xariir was paralyzed with pain of his own. He could do nothing for himself but most importantly he could do nothing for Mayxaano, whose tears were rolling down her cheeks, unabated. Had they been in a house or a less conspicuous corner, had there been a baby to distract the dangerously damning public, he would have dared to hold her, to console and comfort her. Fortunately for Mayxaano though—because crying in public was also tantamount to total shame—no one was paying attention.

Mayxaano, who had learned to cage her memories, was in a complete melt down. She thought the painful memories had been numbed by time, but now this reunion with Xariir opened up old wounds. The floodgates of memory tore the lid off and Mayxaano wept inconsolably.

The four young teens would gather in a house, turn on what

was then a new phenomenon (a radio) in Somalia, a nation
that was itself only five to six years old. They would tune into
a new genre called *heeso* that was superbly rhythmic but poetic in merit, close all the windows and doors, and listen with
ecstasy. At the beginning, only the boys would sing along with
the radio but in time, they all learned to let loose. When the
station host would move on to another program and the songs
stopped, Mayxaano would sing a solo that would soar so high
into the heavens that all souls would feel as though they were
seated somewhere in the summit of Saturn. "My God, your
voice has been sent from heaven," they would all attest.

But Xariir's singing wasn't far behind. His voice rang clear
and, like Mayxaano's, was glorious and affable. The other
two, Abyan and Bilaal, were less gifted, but shared the
same invisible stage and bravely sang along, causing all of
them eventually to roar with laughter. Undeniably, each one
had a hand in the talent pool they all toyed with. They enjoyed
each other's company and even permitted themselves to pass
around love notes. These notes, of course, were written in
the form of the poetic songs heard on the radio. Each two
were secretly in love with the other two. The two girls, though
younger, were a bit more patient and savvy, for they would
candidly tell one another that a pure passion was passing
through their veins and would not deny the fact that the boys
were the conduit for it all.

At that time in Somalia, one would not dare to even put a
foot in the door of a girl's house, let alone be inside singing,
unsupervised. Thus it was the luck of the two cousin boys from
Mogadishu who had traveled to Ceerigaabo to find two fine,
young ladies, as the girls would have you call them, whose
mothers would come home late, for they were being forced
to hustle outside for a living—one for pennies and the other

for bundles of money. Mayxaano's mother sold services in semi-servitude by washing clothes and feeding and caring for the children of the well-to-do most afternoons and into the evenings. And her father had passed away. Abyan's mother, on the other hand, was much better off. She had a wholesale business of her own but would still work 16 long hours a day. She was a very independent woman whose husband was away in *tacabir*.

The boys, however, were from a well-off family. They were staying in a huge house next to Abyan's that Bilaal's father and Xiriir's uncle had built for his "sought after, future second wife."

It all started when Xariir and Bilaal began sitting on the front steps, sporting the newest and most popular instrument from the "advanced world," a radio. They would turn on the "*aalad*" to the max as they took it upon themselves to share this new form of poetic entertainment with the two ravishing teenage girls next door.

Xariir and Bilaal began the entertainment by first blasting the music from the windows of their house, and then eventually summoning enough courage to bring the instrumental beast (*aalad*) into the open. The music was alluringly lyrical and moving. Though at first they would not admit it, the girls next door would listen through a slightly opened window or door until they too summoned the courage to venture out to the front steps.

Mayxaano, who would visit her best friend Abyan every day, sometimes even twice a day, was the first to pass pleasantries to the worldly boys on the stoop. After several days of carefully chosen greetings, the girls finally invited the boys and their *aalad* into Abyan's house. Rest assured that no one in the neighborhood ever saw them either entering or leaving. And there, the remainder of their story ensued. A secret, yet

not-so-secret, teenage passion bloomed.

To be fair though, their summer activities were not solely limited to flirtation. They soon moved on to a more serious task of collecting poetry. At the same time, they pooled their talent and began to tutor the poor children from the neighborhood in Math, Arabic, English, and even Somali poetry. These were the "undeserving" children who had been passed by unnoticed or rather blatantly ignored by their neighbors.

Then one day in August 1964, they realized that the summer vacation was about to end. Approaching their last tutoring session, Xariir, Bilaal, Mayxaano and Abyan decided to make their last class ceremonious and cheerful.

On a Thursday evening, Bilaal addressed the gathering by telling one of his best stories of a very special bird. While flying across the country, the bird spotted a raging wildfire, consuming a nesting area of another species of migrating birds. Without hesitation the bird swooped down to a nearby well, wet her wings, and flew back to the wildfire, sprinkling drops of water on the raging flames. The story was a classic, one of proverbial goodwill exercised in futility.

Mayxaano was her usual self, as captivating as ever. The night before, she had finished reading *A Thousand and One Arabian Nights*, which she, herself, orally translated into Somali for the children. They were entranced by her recitation.

Abyan performed admirably by using pounds and pounds of empty snail shells, to demonstrate the power of compounding.

Finally, Xariir tapped into a nationalism that was alive and well in Somalia then by launching into a long story, laced with patriotism, topping it with one of Cabdullahi Qarshe's best and most popular songs. He punctuated it with a bit of his own narration in how this humble, under-educated man became a maverick and major music icon. Xariir went on to share how

Cabdullahi Qarshe, while living in Aden, had invented Somali music altogether by borrowing the seed melody from Indian and Arabic pools.

His eager audience listened with rapt attention as Xariir explained how, in 1948, both Yemen and northern Somalia were victimized by the colonial yoke of British rule. Though radio programs were in British control, it aired Somali, Arabic and Hindu languages. The Somali segment consisted of only the news followed by a short time of Somali poetry, with no Somali music or songs, whereas both the Arabs and the Indians indulged themselves in a feverish melodic feast. "Mind you," he said, "Cabdullahi Qarshe was trained in Aden in a religious school to become an Imam, yet repatriated back to Somalia with no more than a single lute and music in his heart. He learned how to play the 'prized' instrument with a mesmerizing baritone voice mostly after he was back in the motherland, making sure that Somalis had their share of the heavenly healing tone. I should remind you, however, how Cabdullahi Qarshe (and please note that I am uttering his whole name, for I am acknowledging how sacred that is to me and it should be to you all, too) composes poetic songs with the most patriotic taste, at times even pleading for the reunification of all Somali-speaking people."

Dadkaa dhawaaqayaa
Dhulkoodaa doonayaa
The people whose voices you are hearing
Desire (freedom) for the (colonized) motherland

As Xariir recited these verses, everybody joined in, enticed by the pathos-laden, patriotic lyrics.

Suddenly the singing was interrupted by a middle-aged woman who burst into the room like a tornado. She stopped at the center of the room, put her hands on her hips, and

surveyed the scene, eyeing each person with an intense scrutiny. There, she fired off the foulest, most vulgar Somali words. And the worst of it was the way she delivered them, though no one knew why. The group later learned that this vile speaking woman was Xiriir and Bilaal's aunt.

"You poor children," she began to purr. "How unfortunate is it that you have had to listen to Midgaan Mayxaano, a maggot among the living, singing for you. Woe to me, and to my brother and sister! Whatever happened to our clan's honor? How on earth can a Midgaan be allowed to curse you with her malicious moan?"

It was as though a haze of sorrow seized them all. A sense of doom descended on the room. Everybody tried to scramble out from under her opprobrium. Some of the children began to weep, some simply sobbed, and others just walked out one by one, hanging their heads low.

The multilayer pain of shame that the words carried seemed unbearable. Every Somali knows "Midgaan" is the worst type of an insult. Anything and everything that is hated, shameful, shied away from or avoided is attributed to or associated with "Midgaan." What is so mystifying is that no one knows why the "Midgaan" is so defiled and demonized. There are Somalis branded as "Midgaans" though they are no different from the rest, and unless someone singles them out as "Midgaans," no one is able tell them apart. Yet they are being subjugated to an infinitely disdainful and degrading assault. Why? It's one of those malevolent mysteries that no one is able to explain.

In the house, minutes ticked away before Bilaal finally stood up, eyes burning from the pain caused by his aunt's vile mouth. He avoided looking at her but clenched his fingers, as though to show his anger and shame.

Slowly, when every child had exited the house and both Abyan and Mayxaano had also left the-by-now-haunted house, Xariir and Bilaal remained with their lunatic, barely lucid aunt, bathed in a haze of shame.

At dawn the next morning, Bilaal's body was found hanging from a tree right in front of the mosque.

In his pocket was a brief note, a daring repudiation of the religious sect: "Why has our society remained silent while fellow citizens are maligned? Why have the acclaimed Sheikhs and clan chiefs not defended the dignity of those defamed as Midgaan? You, the men of the mosque, you who have been entrusted with 'God's wisdom,' have tolerated a mountain of social injustice inflicted upon Somali minority clans. Thus, as a person, I could not, would not, cannot and will not live within a society stripped of its human decency and the dignity of life. I, therefore, bid you farewell!"

Now that Mayxaano had Xariir, Bilaal's best friend and cousin in her presence, she was a mess. All the pain in her past began to gnaw at her heart. She wanted to tell and tell it all and she wanted to ask and ask it all, but would she? Tears sailed down her cheeks. Though it seemed like an eternity, only minutes passed before she finally fainted. In seconds, the people around and in the Daalo restaurant whom she had just chastised for not being compassionate enough to care for scuffling teenagers gathered around her. Some ran in search of an ambulance (mind you, there were no telephones in the entire city of Burco). Some rushed about, bringing back bowls of water to dampen her face. Some preferred to fan her with their bare hands and still others just shouted frivolous instructions, making noise but no sense.

When she fell, Xariir immediately slunk to the ground

and—ignoring the cultural taboo—cradled her head in his lap while making sure that she remained covered and protected from the invading eyes of lecherous fools.

Soon the wailing siren of a speeding van plagued the air. Ten yards outside the corral, the ambulance came to an abrupt halt. The group of men who only hours ago had seemed to be Mayxaan's enemy now lifted and carried her gingerly. They placed her gently onto the waiting gurney. The ambulance closed its doors and took off urgently. The siren soared again, and with distance lost its intensity, finally fading altogether.

The Mayxaano Chronicles:
Dissonance

About 1:30 p.m., a group of Ceerigaabo soccer team members streamed into Daalo restaurant in Burco and were greeted with, "Dalmar, Dalmar, Dalmar," followed by a round of applause and whistles. Soon a mob of well-wishers, who had either watched the game Ceerigaabo had won against the much-favored powerhouse Hargeisa or had heard about it, swarmed them.

The star of the game, Dalmar, was in the middle of it, taking it all in. As people young and old competed to touch him or get his attention for a second, a soccer ball landed on a table a few feet away, where a man of means and his female companion were having lunch. The woman, who was assuredly his date, although no one would dare to call it so lest it offend "religious sensitivity," suffered blots on her clothing from the soup's splash. Incensed, the man jumped to his feet to grab the offending ball, but he was no match for an agile 12-year-old boy, who scooped it up, ran for a breach in the fence, slipped through it, and cut right across the street. He turned around, laughing.

The man of means was, as a matter of fact, a Somali National Army lieutenant. Let it be known that, only a decade or so old, the Soviet-armed Somali National Army was one of the most powerful, envied, and feared militaries on the continent of Africa. Thus, anyone who was fortunate enough to wear its uniform would bathe in its pride, but most of the awe was reserved for the officers. And this lieutenant knew it.

With his decorated uniform, the lieutenant ran after the little boy. Pretending indifference, the boy waited and waited, but when the trained officer tried to tackle him, the tiny boy ducked and the officer flew past.

Head-on, the officer collided with a man pushing a wheelbarrow full of fruit and vegetables for sale. His pristine uniform sustained substantial blotches of red, green, and yellow pulp.

As though he were about to salute a highly decorated, higher-ranking officer, the obviously offended officer stood still, lowered his gaze and then lowered it some more to his feet. Like a robot, he mechanically turned to look at his shoulder where his credentials were pinned. Then he walked briskly back to the restaurant and sat down.

To help him rid the stains from his shirt, his companion reached out to brush it with her bare hand.

"Leave it alone, leave it alone," the officer grumbled. "I will have my serviceman take care of it. It's the federal government's property… That small rat! He isn't going to get away with it. Just watch. I am going to send my unit out to apprehend him. My nation will not tolerate this miscreant type, minor or major."

Irritated, it seemed, the woman said, "He is just a child. He is just having some fun."

"Having fun, having fun?! You call that having fun? No, no that is not a child having fun." He stood up and pointed to his uniform. "This is a dishonor and a disgrace to the nation. You know where and when a nation falls from grace? It starts here, here," he answered himself. "That's exactly what happens: that a rascal like him would humiliate an esteemed officer in public." His shouting attracted the attention of the next table, the Ceerigaabo soccer team and its crowd. "Let us go," he ordered his company.

Before the words were out of his mouth, however, he saw the boy with the ball making his way into the restaurant. The officer went after him.

The boy made a beeline to Dalmar. "Hey, Dalmar," he began, keeping an eye on the menacing looking officer, "I was so impressed with your game yesterday, and wanted to know…"

"Whoa, whoa," others interrupted, blocking the officer's way. "Come on. He is a child, can you not see?"

The dissonance echoed.

"I don't care. This 'child' damaged national property and has to pay a price or at least his family must," the officer responded. He pointed to the splotches on his otherwise immaculate uniform. Not once did he even hint that his female companion had suffered the same "dishonor."

"I am quite confident that our esteemed National Army officer can let him off with a fair warning," said Dalmar. "Believe me, I understand that this is a major breach of an officer's honor, sir. But he's just a child playing with a ball. Can you let it be?"

From behind Dalmar's back, the boy stuck his tongue out at the officer. The officer, who had seemed sold on the idea of letting him go for a second, lost his temper. He went after the boy again. None of the team had seen the boy taunting the officer and once more stood in the way. The boy darted back out of the restaurant and across the road.

Virtually frothing from the mouth, the officer aimed his fury at Dalmar. "You son-of-a-not-so-good-mother, you meant to distract me all along. I knew you were with that rascal from the beginning."

Dalmar's older teammates, who felt responsible for him, stepped in. In their politest manner, they told the officer to mind his own business and to leave the minor to his, and Dalmar to his, as well.

On the patio, the standoff was attracting a bit of a crowd when a young man and another uniformed military man appeared at the corner. Disappointed, one of Dalmar's friends said, "Here we go. Now we have to wrestle with armed Somali National Forces. Don't they have an enemy to watch?" Every step the uniformed man and companion took towards the restaurant raised the tension.

But the seething lieutenant took one step back, then another, and finally went back to his seat. When they were close enough, it was clear that the military man now approaching outranked the irascible officer. The seething officer jumped to his feet and firmly planted his feet on the ground, raising a stiff hand to his forehead. The superior officer let his cowering subordinate wag his tail, like a jackal greeting an alpha female. He put the ireful one in his place by simply being on the scene and taking the salute not a second too soon.

The arriving officer enveloped Dalmar in a bear hug, lifted him off the ground onto his shoulders, and pretended to run off with him. The rest of the team played along, pretending that they were not going to let him take their most valuable player by blocking the officer each way he turned. Wise to the game, the officer put Dalmar down. Forehead to forehead, he placed both of his hands on his shoulders, then on his cheeks, and said, "Dalmar, Dalmar, Dalmar, I am so proud of you and have always been, but this time I am not alone. The entire city of Ceerigaabo and the whole Sanaag region are, too."

Dalmar's teammates began to chant "Dalmar, Dalmar, Dalmar." It did not take long for the others around the restaurant patio to join in. "Dalmar, Dalmar, Dalmar."

Now the outranked officer slipped through the chanting

crowd like a feral cat, his companion trailing him. At the corner, he looked back as though making sure that he was not being followed.

Everyone was about to take a seat when Dalmar noticed the young man accompanying the military man. "Oh, my goodness gracious, what are you doing here, Ayaanle? I thought you were away in Ceerigaabo," he said, embracing his friend.

The officer beamed with a double pride. "Ayaanle has told me that the whole city of Ceerigaabo was glued to the radio to follow you, and with all the hollering and hooting, most lost their voices. You guys were magical. For the first time in our history, the whole city was in the streets dancing, I am told. The only missing troupe was you guys. But no worries; I am sure we can repeat it once you're back from Mogadishu."

Around them the waiter wailed, "*Waar sagaal laydha ah keen* [nine cups of tea outside], *waar sagaal laydha ah keen, waar sagaal laydha ah keen*." The waiter took one more look at the Ceerigaabo team's table and said, "*Waar sagaal daayo baaldi halkan keen* [never mind nine cups of tea, bring a whole bucket of tea over here]." The waiter adjusted his counting chant to reflect the crowd.

"But, Abti[1]," Dalmar said, "wouldn't you say that all the ecstasy will be gone by the time we are back from Mogadishu?"

Some of his teammates were nodding in agreement when the second youngest of the team, 19-year-old Kayse, asked, "What is the matter, Dalmar? You think Ceerigaabo's love will dry up by the time we are back from the capital?"

Everybody laughed.

"Well, there is one way to avoid it all," Dalmar said. "We don't have to go to the second leg of the competition. We just

1 Uncle

go back to Ceerigaabo before the love dries up. And when we are asked why we are back before the tournament is over, we tell them, 'Listen. You don't love us enough. And to make the matter worse, we don't know whether we are going to win in Mogadishu. So we thought we would make sure we bring the victory back to collect the admiration you owe us.'" Laughter interrupted the speech.

"Half-baked victory," someone said. More laughter ensued, but louder.

"Right," said Kayse. "We never knew what winning was. So now that we have half of a victory, we will always say, 'Remember when we won the qualifying leg of a tournament?'"

"To milk it as best as we can," Dalmar said.

"See, it works, Dalmar. No, no, actually we will never mention a qualifying leg," Kayse clarified. "We will only talk about when we beat Hargeisa." More laughter followed.

"OK, OK, I got it, you guys," Dalmar said. "Lay off me now, people, would you?"

During the laughter and light clapping, a tray of tea cups had arrived.

"Guys, it's time for lunch. What are you going to order besides tea? I am going to leave my salary on the table today," said the officer.

"Lunch is waiting for us at the center hosting us," said a teammate.

"Abti, we are all set," said Dalmar. "It's our last lunch in Burco. So we want to be there. We are leaving for Mogadishu at 7:00 a.m. tomorrow and some are saying it may be midnight tonight. Right, guys?"

"Right, Dalmar," Kayse said but winked to the guy next to him and whispered, "Dalmar wants to see how many howling girls will show up at the center to see him at lunch."

Dalmar, who heard the laughter coming from the next chair, said, "I heard that!"

"No, you didn't," said Kayse.

"Yes, I did; something about girls."

A roar of laughter went around.

"And speaking of girls, I am serious now," said Dalmar, "Does anybody know the name of the woman who started it all?"

"You guys are kidding me," said Ayaanle. "You guys have no clue who lit the fire that spurred you into the historic victory? If I were you, I would have started my victory dance with her."

"Listen, Ayaanle, no offense, my man, but you don't know what it felt like to win. So yes, I, Dalmar Cali Faarax, was dancing but I was not alone. To be honest, though, I would have danced much the same if I were alone." Again the rest of his friends laughed.

Ayaanle held Dalmar by the elbow and pulled him aside.

"Listen, the female voice that started it all was none other than the incomparable Mayxaano. Remember our hero back in Ceerigaabo? Remember her?"

"Of course I do. How could I ever forget her?" He paused to process what he had heard. "Hold it, hold it, you always avoided talking about her when we were young. How is…"

"Listen, listen," interrupted Ayaanle, "leave that childish behavior of mine alone and hear me out…"

"I will, but before I let you take back the term, I am not so sure if you know how much I miss her and what she means to me."

"I don't, but I can guess," said Ayaanle. "Anyway, she was the person who started the 'Dalmar, Dalmar, Dalmar' chant. My uncle was sitting next to her and told me that the whole stadium reverberated with 'Dalmar, Dalmar, Dalmar.' That was when the coach realized that he had to put you in the game or risk a riot. And look what happened; you not only made history but made us all proud."

"I have to tell you, Ayaanle, that I am playing this game because of her."

"I knew that she taught us a lot but what does she have to do with your soccer game?"

"Are you kidding me? Everything, everything. By the way, when that whole group of hers sang to us the last time…" He trailed off.

"See, I was not misremembering it. She did sing that last night she was in Ceerigabo with us," Ayaanle said.

"What?"

"Nothing; I was talking to myself. Yes, Mayxaano sang that night. And she wasn't alone."

"No, no, she wasn't. Remember Xariir also sang? Remember Abyan, who tried her best? Well, you know where I am going with that. And, and, and of course Bilaal…" Dalmar trailed off once again.

"Wow, what a time we…"

"Guys," the officer interrupted, "it is lunch time and I don't think you two are going to be done soon. So why don't you let the team go?" He turned to the team and said, "Hey, team, don't wait for Dalmar. If you trust me—well, you have to so long as the nation does anyway—I will bring him back soon enough to see him say his goodbye to the crowd waiting outside the gate."

"Are you sure?" asked someone.

"I will try my best," said the officer in the midst of roaring laughter.

The team ambled out of the restaurant, heading to their housing a quarter mile away.

"*Waar sagaal laydha ah keen, waar sagaal laydha ha keen, waar sagaal laydha ah keen.*" The waiter came closer.

The officer waved for him.

"What are you going to order?" the waiter asked.

The officer pointed to Ayaanle and then Dalmar.

"What do you have for lunch?"Ayaanle asked.

"The same as yesterday or the day before, but special for you guys, the soup is free," he said.

The officer laughed and Ayaanle and Dalmar followed. It was amusing how the waiter aptly deployed his sword of sarcasm. They all knew what he had for lunch: lamb, camel, goat, and sheep, and sauced rice and pasta. And it is customary in Somalia that if you are having lunch, no matter what, there should be a bowl of free soup.

Ayaanle ordered camel meat, boiled with cabbage, potatoes, onion, basil, and sauced rice, a typical northern Somali meal, but Dalmar asked for sauced rice and grilled lamb.

"Listen," the waiter said, "I am not sure where you are from and who taught you about 'grilled' lamb and all. But this is Burco and we all order the same food from the same menu."

They all laughed again.

"OK, OK," Dalmar responded. "You won. Just make it lamb. Cook it whichever way you wish. Just bring me some lamb. I gather you have no quarrel with my side order, sauced rice, right?"

"So there and so ordered," the waiter said. He disappeared into the belly of the restaurant.

"What a man with a whip of words," said Ayaanle.

"He's just a kid," the officer said. "He is known around here for his sharp, incisive tongue. So watch yourselves. A lot of people fall victim to his sarcasm. He fights a lot but fights well. You should have seen how he humiliated not one, not two, but three schoolboy brats of your age this morning. He literally fed one from the dust and dirt right there. You see where the earth is still disturbed." He pointed out the marks on the ground.

The officer went inside, paid the bill, came out, and said, "See you guys later."

"See you later," said Dalmar.

"OK, Dalmar. Tell me, what were you saying about Mayxaano?"

"Well, the fact that I am playing this game, the fact that I am a good student, and the fact that I am a friend of yours are all due to the seeds she sowed," said Dalmar. "I had no clue of her whereabouts until you wrote me about your encounter with her in Sheikh. Boy, I was glad that you saw her. And from the little you said in the letter, I could tell you were as excited about it as I was hearing about it."

"Have you ever wondered where she was and what became of her?"

"For God's sake, yes. But what on earth do you expect me to say when you, my best friend, the only person that I could have confided in, always avoided the subject? I thought that somehow, somewhere, I did something wrong. And you were not willing to go there with me."

Now that Ayaanle knew what he had been avoiding and why, he felt guilty. His grandmother had told to him never, never talk about Mayxaano to anyone, but the pain of keeping a lid on it that long was heavier than he had thought. And he was not alone. His friend Dalmar had suffered as much if not more. To keep himself from crying, he bit his lower lip, but was helped in time by the waiter who came back with his chant, "*Waar sagaal layadha ah keen, waar sagaal lyaydha ah keen, waar sagaal laydha ah keen,*" unloading plates of food off a tray at a nearby table.

"Hey, your lip is bleeding," Dalmar yelled.

Ayaanle pulled a handkerchief from his pants pocket and went to the hose on the wall outside the restaurant. He washed himself and patted the cut with the handkerchief but the bleeding continued. He returned and asked the waiter for cold water, though he expected none. He knew there was neither a refrigerator nor a first aid kit.

Suddenly someone tapped him on the shoulder. When he looked up, a man handed him a cup of ice in a towel and said, "Here, son. Hold it to the cut." Taking the needed gift, his gaze lingered on the man giving it. Something about the man's face was vaguely familiar.

"Hey, young man, you have to put the ice on the cut," the man ordered him. "Hurry." He looked at Dalmar. "Hey, I know you! You're the man who massacred Hargeisa yesterday! That was a hell of a game. Man, I have never enjoyed a game as much as I did yesterday. How on earth did you learn how to play like that at such a young age?"

"Thanks so much," said Dalmar. "That means a lot to me but it has been a long road and a lot of investment from a lot of people that I am not sure I will ever be able to repay." Dalmar looked away and asked Ayaanle, "Did it stop?"

Ayaanle tapped his lower lip with the iced towel. "I think it did."

"Let us wait for the food. And this time, please don't chew before the camel meat arrives," Dalmar joked.

"Yeah, thanks for your kind words, pal." Ayaanle looked at the man inquisitively.

"This victory was overdue," the man continued. "I was in Ceerigaabo a decade ago and met great kids as well as a friend for life. You two probably were in your mothers' laps at the time. Hey, I am sorry but you two eat before your lunch gets cold."

He was walking by barking orders to waiters, making it quite apparent that he was the manager, when a man called out, "Hey, Xariir, Xariir, wait, wait."

Ayaanle, who was not sure he heard the name called right, froze for a second, looked at Dalmar, and saw him react the same way.

"Dalmar," Ayaanle asked. "Did I hear that right? He said Xariir, didn't he?"

"I think so."

"Yes, yes, it's him, it's him! Did you see how I was staring at him? Did you notice the gap between his front teeth? I was wondering why his face was familiar."

"I think so, too," Dalmar said. "There aren't many Somalis called Xariir."

"I can assure you that I have not met anyone else called Xariir since," said Ayaanle.

"And he just said to us that he was in Ceerigaabo a decade ago."

"Right," said Ayaanle.

They overheard a man inquiring about a woman who had fainted on the restaurant's patio earlier that morning.

"She is fine," the manager replied. "She had a dizzy spell. The doctors said she is anemic."

Dalmar could not hold back his excitement. He called, "Xariir."

The man turned around and said, "Yes?"

They jumped to their feet.

"You were in Ceerigaabo ten years ago, you said? Did you teach neighborhood kids that summer?" asked Ayaanle

"Sure, I did, and I wasn't alone."

"I can't believe it, I just can't believe it," said Dalmar, tears in his eyes, grabbing the man in a hug. He laughed. "You probably think we are lunatics but I can assure you there is a reason for all of this."

"We are the two youngest of a troop of neighborhood kids that you tutored that summer," said Ayaanle.

"No, no, no. I can't believe this either," said Xariir, placing one hand on Dalmar and the other on Ayaanle.

"Xariir, you have no idea how much you guys changed me," Dalmar said.

"How so?" Xariir asked, grinning from ear to ear.

"Let me jog your memory. Do you remember a boy in your tutoring sessions with a make-shift soccer ball, made of old stuffed socks?"

"Wooooow. Don't tell me you're the agile, energetic boy everybody called Dooli because of how tiny you were? I can't believe it. I can't believe the tiny 'Mouse' is this fine young man with muscles. Irony, I know. I saw your talent all along but how is it that you are already here with such honed skills?"

"The name is gone. You see, I am not a mouse anymore. So, the nickname Doolli lost its luster. Irony also has no place in the game of soccer, you might agree."

"When I think about your early childhood agility, plus the skill you have developed to master and manipulate the ball, you are right, irony has no place there." He turned to Ayaanle and said, "And you?"

"He was the youngest of us. I was the second youngest. Remember the one with the notebook that we used to call 'The Kitaab'?" asked Dalmar.

"My, my. 'The Holy Book.' Don't tell me this is Ayaanle?"

"Yep, it's me, Xariir."

Xariir offered his hand, and they hugged.

"He is still with books; only they are not so holy anymore," said Dalmar. "He is after them like the aardvark is after termites."

"His thoughts are holy to me as long as he is feeding his mind with what it needs the most: books," said Xariir.

"Amen to that," said Ayaanle.

"Xariir, honestly, all this talent would not be possible if it were not for you guys, particularly both you and Mayxaano," Dalmar said.

"Please go on and tell me how. I am a selfish being. I can't help but be an addendum to your miraculous success?"

Dalmar began to narrate a tale he had never told before, not even to his best friend Ayaanle. He related how he came to Mayxaano's tutorial classes wherever they were held, in a house, under a shade of a tree, or at her humble home, always with his makeshift soccer ball made of old socks in his armpit. One day, he arrived with bloody feet. When she asked what had happened, he simply said that he had been playing in bare feet. Here he was no different than the rest of the neighborhood kids. None had shoes for a soccer game. But Dalmar played on gravel streets where small rocks were scattered everywhere. Mayxaano washed his wound, wrapped a clean cloth on it, held his hand, and walked a quarter of a mile to the Darista Ceerigaabo. She told him to always play soccer there, in the soft green grass. It was safer.

"When I began playing there, the fear of hurting myself went away. And at 5:00 p.m. every afternoon, Mayxaano would come to see me play with kids, most of them older. I felt valued," said Dalmar.

One day Mayxaano brought two young men with her and all three watched him play until another boy came with a new soccer ball.

Everyone on the field ran to the new boy, who soon was deciding who was allowed to join him in play. The boy with a new soccer ball picked everybody but Dalmar. When Dalmar protested, the boy told him that he did not want the ugly, make-shift ball in the same field with his as though it were going to contaminate either the ground or the new ball. When Dalmar said he was going to throw his away, the boy said OK. But when Dalmar did as he was told, the boy laughed at him. Then he said that he wasn't going to let the feet that touched the stuffed ball touch his ball anyway. Dalmar was beyond distress and began to cry. Mayxaano and her friends tried to reason with the boy with the ball but to no avail. So they took Dalmar with them and left.

"Two days later, about five in the afternoon, Mayxaano and her two friends showed up at the soccer field and found me sitting alone and still in distress, watching the rest of my friends enjoying a game. Xariir, you were the one who approached me. You asked me to guess what you had in your hand. I was in no mood to play a guessing game. You stood right in front of me and offered me a new soccer ball. When I still did not move a finger, you handed me that ball and said, 'Yes, it's yours.' When I still didn't move, Mayxaano said, 'Dalmar, it's true. It's yours.' I did take the ball and I am here to tell you the rest. By the way, the ball was not just any soccer ball but *'abu cudbi,'* a soccer ball made of cotton, the most durable of all."

"I remember when Mayxaano said, 'It's yours,' you snatched the ball from my hands and bolted away," Xariir said. "No thanks or any such thing." They all laughed. "Seriously, I remember how pleased we were when we saw how happy you were with the ball."

"That ball changed me and changed how the world reacted to me. First of all, every boy on that same soccer field suddenly wanted to be my friend. But as time went on, my ball outlasted that boy's ball as well as every other one. Oh, by the way, the same boy is on my team now…"

"And he isn't able to keep you out now?" interrupted Xariir.

"No, and he has not been for a long time anyway. Remember my ball outlasted his. Oh, where was I?" Dalmar choked up. "Xariir, I did not thank you then and I don't believe I will ever be able to as much as you deserve. I owe you a great debt of gratitude. That much I know."

"Wow," Ayaanle joined in, "we have been friends ever since that year, yet I did not know half of this."

"This is the greatest gift ever," said Xariir. "You guys made my day."

"Why don't you tell Xariir your story, Ayaanle? Everybody knows you are the poet-writer, the one who molds words with melody..."

"That is Cumar Dhuule, the man I am writing about. You are mixing me up with a legend," interrupted Ayaanle.

"You see how old he is? He is already writing a book," said Dalmar.

"Yes, I was one of those children who were so fortunate to have you as a tutor that memorable summer," said Ayaanle. "I was also fortunate enough to live next door to Mayxaano, so we had a special bond. We still live in close proximity today. She is a math and literature teacher at Sheikh High School and I am a student there."

"Sure, I was pissed when he wrote me a letter two years ago, when he had arrived at Sheikh High School and who did he say? None other than Her Majesty Mayxaano," said Dalmar.

"I can't believe my short stay is bringing all this gift of joy. You guys have no idea how much I needed it. By the way, you won't believe who else was here this morning."

"Who?" asked both Ayaanle and Dalmar at the same time.

"Let me finish. For a long time, I really had a hard time re-membering much of the good in that summer that you are so aptly referencing. I know; I know most of it was a great fun. But." He hesitated. "There was a bit of a sour note at the end, too. For sure, we can see today that the best superseded the blemishes. And you are dusting off whatever is left of the spoiler residue. But I have to talk about what you have been avoiding. Yes, Bilaal was lost that summer, and yes, he killed himself.

"Not to assign any blame to all the great things we achieved together, but I should let you know why we lost him. We lost him to an accumulation of social illnesses. Some were the Somalis' cursed caste system we encountered the last night of our tutorial summer session, but others were colonial history. What most people did not know was that Bilaal and I were partially raised in Kenya during its darkest days in history, the middle of the Mau Mau war. The British colony's anger as well as racism was at its peak at that time, though many would have you believe otherwise. It so happened that Bilaal had a 7-year-old Kikuyu neighbor friend, a little boy of the same age. I remember a day when Bilaal came home running like a hunted deer. We learned later that he was playing outside with his friend when a British teenager, who had moved from South Africa, showed up with a gun. The boy put the gun on the Kikuyu child's forehead and said, 'If I ever see you in our neighborhood, you fucking *kaffir*, I am going to shoot you dead. You monkeys have been killing our people and we have had enough of you.'

"Days later, Bilaal and his friend saw his friend's father chased down the road with a gun by the same boy and his father, followed by the horror of hearing *pop, pop, pop, pop*. Next thing they knew, his friend's father was on the ground, bleeding to death. He was shot four times. A week after, our cook, Kikuyu too, came home bleeding. On his way to work he had been shot by the colonial Kenyan Police, who accused him of being a Mau Mau sympathizer. My uncle, Bilaal's father, took the cook to a nomadic medicine man, for he was unable to trust the medical staff at the closest hospital. We never heard from our cook again. No one knew whether he survived or succumbed to his injury. When my uncle tried to find him, the nomad was nowhere to be found. He had moved on.

"Bilaal lived with those nightmares all the years that followed. He became overly sensitive to any kind of social injustice, but in particular the caste system in our country. He was not living with white discrimination anymore but black on black or worse Somali on Somali. He could not process that. What no one knew was the severity of it until it consumed him and killed him."

Xariir noticed that a hush had descended on the table when the waiter's words, "*Waar sagaal laydha ah keen, waar sagaal laydha ah keen, waar sagaal laydha ah keen*," broke the tension. The waiter stopped at their table with plates wrapped in a piece of cloth and moved on with his chant.

"I have to take this lunch to someone special who is expecting me in a few minutes. Frankly though, it would put a remarkable stamp on this reunion if you guys go with me. But for now, don't ask any questions until we get there," said Xariir.

"Sure, why not?" asked Dalmar.

"Of course," Ayaanle followed.

"Don't worry about the bill, I will take care of it," Xariir said.

"No, no, it's already taken care of," said Ayaanle.

"OK, then let us go," Xariir said, gripping the cloth-wrapped food.

Before they walked out of the restaurant, he called the waiter and told him that he was going to be away for the evening. The job of running a business in Somalia was, and is, a 24-hour responsibility, short of the sleeping time. Over the bridge, they walked the short distance north to Burco's main hospital. Once they approached the all-female unit, Xariir told the other two to stay behind but wait for his signal to follow, one at a time. He proceeded into a warehouse-like hall, populated by row after row of beds for patients.

"Hey, I have a feeling that you are well," Xariir said to a woman in a curtained off space. "If not, I have with me what the doctor should have prescribed."

The woman inside the tent said, "I don't believe you, Xariir. Prove it to me."

Xariir waved back to the two young friends behind him to follow. "OK, OK, brace yourself, lady," he said, as Dalmar raced to catch up with him. Xariir and Dalmar were closing in when the woman, who had measured the distance from their footsteps, pulled open the curtain. She recognized Dalmar and let out a shriek that echoed through the hall. The same 'sick woman in bed' jumped off and wrapped her arms around him.

Xariir, who sensed that Dalmar had no clue what he had gotten himself into, dropped it on him: "Dalmar, if you have been looking for your idol Mayxaano, make sure you don't let her go again. She is in your hands."

Dalmar's steel-like legs quivered. Mayxaano tried to brace him with her body but out of the corner of her left eye saw her protégé Ayaanle, who dropped a cluster of papers and was running towards her. Ayaanle, Dalmar, and Mayxaano formed a unit. Mayxaano tried her best to hold it together but the other two let their emotions address the audience.

The unit's patients propped themselves up with pillows to watch the reunion.

"What is this?" asked Mayxaano. "Have I finally managed to break through the mold of Somali's male ego? *Nimanka Soomaaliyeed ma ooyaanna ha iga hadho*. Let the proverbial

'Somali men don't cry' die in me." She laughed, loosening her embrace but still holding onto Ayaanle in one hand and Dalmar in the other.

Four or five feet away, Xariir put the food down on a table and picked up the cluster of papers Ayaanle had dropped. He looked at the first page, then another and another, went back to the first, hesitated, harrumphed, and said, "The first is a letter addressed to Her Majesty Mayxaano. It says, 'Hello, Mayxaano. You may not remember much about us and wouldn't recognize our faces today but we do remember you—we are the neighborhood children you endured so much pain for in order to prepare them for life. Fifty-three strong and all over the nation, we are all in schools with the exception of our dear friend Indhadeero. We lost her last year when a car she was in rolled over on the highway between Burco and Mogadishu. God bless her, we miss her, but she was called early to attend to a duty we dare not define. We also almost lost Addeeca to what you used to call "The Invented Enemy of Young Women," an early, arranged marriage. But no worries, she is going to graduate with us this coming school year because we have been tutoring her at her home. And do you know what? For the first time both the school authorities and her husband allowed all we asked and fought for, including taking the exam with us, which in itself is historic.

"'Now, to let you know, Ayaanle came to join us back in Ceerigaabo for our fourth anniversary reunion, which we call "Summer Loyalty to her Majesty Mayxaano," to honor what you taught us best. We decided that every summer we are going to collect the neighborhood kids and tutor them. That, we thought, would be the least we could do to keep the legacy you left alive. Our hope is to inspire others as you did for us.

"'Ayaanle also made us aware that your love for Somali

poetry lives on. It lives on in us, too. When he told us that you would like to collect a specific group of songs, the romantic type beginning with Cumar Dhuule, we agreed as well as promised to collaborate with you and Ayaanle.

"'Lastly, it will be remiss of us if we don't ask a favor of you. We want you in Ceerigaabo next summer. Mayxaano, you are so dear to us that we are either going to find you or you are going to come to see us. We believe that we are making a case for ourselves because you are one and we are an army. Don't delay our demand or else…

"'Sincerely,

"'Your inspired, now grown-up Ceerigaabo neighborhood kids. Love and forever love.'"

Mayxaano let her tears loose, but this time it was neither for pain nor blame.

The Vulture has Landed

Ayaan made a hiding place for her 9-year-old sister in the attic of their house. She filled up most of the space with rusty bicycles, old tires, and worn out clothes, leaving barely enough room to open and close the door itself. In the back of that mess, she left a small space for a mattress with two blankets and a pillow. At the entrance, finally, she hung a bloodstained women's cloth to conceal the door.

When she finished, she called her sister from the living room where Caataye, her husband of two months, had been tutoring the little girl. Ayaan held her sister's hands apart and pulled her into an embrace. "My precious sister," she said to the young girl leaning against her chest, "listen very carefully to what I am telling you and promise to do what I tell you to do. You do know a promise must be kept, don't you?"

"Yes, my sister," said Amran, arms around her sister's waist. "I know that if you promise something you should live up to it, and I promise to do what you ask me to do."

"Then listen, dear girl. I have finished fixing up the place for you. From now on, you are going to sleep there every night. I have already shown you how to go in and out of it. If there's anything else you need, let me know and if we can afford it, I will bring it to you. Are you listening to me, my dear?"

"Yes, sister." Amran lifted her head from her sister's chest and stared at the floor.

Ayaan looked away for a second, then peered back at her sister, trying to lift the child's gaze to hers. She knew that

Amran was smarter and more mature than most children of her age; but she had to make sure that Amran understood and remembered exactly what she had to say.

"Now, sweetie," she said, "I am going to teach you some code words that only you, Caataye, and I will know. Any time I say, 'The vulture has landed,' it means it's time for you to hide. So if you are not already in your hiding place, you must run as fast as you can to get there. And you must not come out until you hear Caataye or me saying, 'It is a bright morning.'"

Ayaan noted that she had scared her sister when Amran asked, "Ayaan, what is going on? Is the militia looking for us?"

Ayaan tried to speak calmly, pushing away her fear that the three of them might be attacked in the middle of the night. "You see, last week, the rebel movement cost the dictator Barre's army some casualties. They broke into a Somali National Security prison and freed three high-ranking officers, all from the north, who had been sentenced to death by hanging. One of them was Cilmi, Caataye's best friend."

Ayaan did not want to explain the situation in detail or show her distress. But she had to let her sister know the danger they were in. She was actually more afraid for her sister than she was for herself and Caataye. The militia was capable of callously raping the child and, for that matter, Ayaan herself right in front of her husband, before wasting them all. She vowed to herself that, by the grace of God, she was going to keep her sister from harm, no matter what.

"My sweetie," she said, "I need you to go into your room and wait for me, so I can have a word with Caataye."

As Amran left for her room, Ayaan stepped out of the kitchen and met Caataye on his way back from the hiding place. He looked furious. He sat next to Ayaan and fired off a torrent of sentences all at once. "Ayaan, why in hell did you hang that thing in the door? Why in God's name choose a bloody cloth to be the first thing that the innocent girl sees in the morning, and the last she sees at night?"

"Caataye—" Ayaan tried to interrupt.

"Why on earth did you not let me know about it before you went ahead?"

"Caataye—" Ayaan tried again.

"When did you do it anyway?"

He was still shooting off when Ayaan raised her voice. "Caa—aa—taayeeee. Calm down, damn it. And at least give me a chance to respond."

Caataye looked away, raised both hands up, brought them down and rested them on his knees.

"First of all this is not human blood," she said, putting a hand on her hip and wagging an index finger in his face.

"How in God's name is a child going to know that?" Caataye erupted.

"Caa-aa-aatayeee! Would you please be a man and let me finish?"

Caataye put his hands on his head and, looking up at the roof, said, "Go ahead, surprise me, and now."

"Just wait a minute then, would you please?" Ayaan yelled. "Second, Taakulo, the butcher woman next door, brought these bloody clothes to me when I asked for them last month. Back then I knew it was going to get worse before it got better, so I tried to be prepared. That's why I chose animal blood, to camouflage the door, hoping anyone with a drop of human decency would be too disgusted to open that door. If that happens, she's safe at least for that day, which could be a lifetime these days. Don't you know, you and she are the only light of life left for me? Every rustle of leaves from a tree at night turns my stomach inside-out, thinking that they have come for you, darling. God only knows how long you'll be with us. But I didn't want to tell you all this because I didn't want you to go off, preaching about the morality that's long been dead in this country of ours—or raise your voice against me, the same way you're doing now. You know," she said, tears gathering in her eyes, "God forbid if these pigs," and then the tears rolled down on her cheeks, "raa-a-pe her… I swear to God, I will kill them all, I will kill them all off, and I will burn the whole damn nation before I go to rest in my grave."

She knew that Caataye usually kept his emotions strictly to himself, just like any Somali man. But Ayaan's sermon seemed to have struck a chord. He grimaced and fought back tears. Then he put his hands around Ayaan, pulled her towards him, and wiped the tears from her eyes with his open palm.

"Darling," he said. "Ayaan, I just got it. I apologize for my ignorance and insensitivity. Your wise judgment has closed the book on this topic. From here on, I will be at your mercy. Now I need some fresh air." He let go of Ayaan and moved lethargically toward the front door.

"Have you forgotten the curfew?" Ayaan asked. She watched him turn away from the door and go to the window, lifting the curtain and scanning the front yard. A drizzling rain was falling; thick clouds covered the sky as far as the eyes could see. He let the curtain fall back in its place, came back to the couch, sat down, and rested his head on the back of the cushion with his hands on his knees.

"This is not rain," he whispered. "These are the tears of the land weeping for justice."

"What have we, the northern people, done to deserve this?" Ayaan lamented. As her grief mounted, it raised her up off the couch and forced itself into words. "Oh God," she said aloud, "why must we live this despicable, disgraceful life?"

shame bullies. He remembered a particular pair of bullies in their neighborhood that they once buried in a pool of contempt.

It was a hot, lazy afternoon. Warsame and Caataye schemed a way to lure the pair of bullies in their neighborhood to a game. They packaged a bundle of pure frozen water that mimicked ice cream cones, then placed themselves where they knew that the pair of bullies hung around. They howled, "Ice cream for sale, ice cream for sale." Once Caataye made sure that the pair of bullies saw him, he turned around and ran, bursting into maximum speed. As though he had seen a ghost, Warsame, too, sprinted after him. The pair of bullies fell for the bait. Around the corner and at the end of the street, Caataye and Warsame reached a half-erected, abandoned basketball court. They stood inside it at the far end of the court. When the pair of bullies reached the entrance, a large fishing net dropped from above, bringing their running to a halt. The pair of bullies stood there and watched "their prey" cross the court, laughing. In a fury of rage, they tried to pull the net out of their way. Instantly, liquids rained down on them. It was a bucket full of animal manure. To make matters worse, a group of neighborhood children, most of whom had been the recipient of their cruelty at one time or the other, were all watching and laughing at them.

Now, Warsame seethed with pain from the memory. It occurred to him that he was in no way closer to resolve the curse of injustice.

Ayaan shivered with pain and shame. She tried to collect herself but could not gather enough strength to heave herself up. The soreness in her body, the violation of her soul, and the filth that had been smeared across her tender heart were all too great to bear.

At first she was certain that she was going to take her life as soon as she could regain control on her feet; but then she remembered her little angel, her innocent sister. She was on the verge of calling Amran from the hiding place, but, just as her lips formed the words, she realized that both the front and the back doors were wide open. Suddenly she recalled that the vulture had said they were going to come back.

With all her effort, she tried to gather herself and salvage whatever was left of the shattered front door to close it. Alas, she could not will her body to sit up. It took all she had to roll onto her side and raise her head a bit above the floor. A wave of nausea washed through her. Her head fell back to the ground. She closed one eye and saw double with the other, closed the one and saw only a blur. She knew that she was drifting into a subconscious zone but fought it off.

Ayaan heard the tumult of cars leaving the house and waited and waited for a human touch. But no one came. She wanted desperately to see her sister but was too scared, so terribly scared, to call out to her.

Finally, she saw Amran tiptoe from her hiding place, then dashing forward toward her. As soon as their eyes met, Amran screamed, "Please, please, God, do not take her away from me! Please, God, do not take her away from me!"

Through a haze, she watched as Amran stopped at the edge of the carpet int he living room. Ayaan was in the middle of it, lying very still. She sensed Amran bending over her and putting her right hand on the base of her throat. Once, too long ago it seemed by now, she knew that Amran had watched her do the same to their mother as she lay on the floor, dying. Now Amran's fingers sought, and found, the pulse of life.

"Ayaan," Amaran exclaimed. "What have they done to you? Oh my God, what have they done to you?"

With a delicate hold, Ayaan followed Amran's command, lifting her head from the floor as Amran placed a pillow under it. Amran ran back to the closet, came back with a towel, soaked it in cold water, and placed it on Ayaan's forehead, as Ayaan had done herself so many times for their mother and other patients she treated as a nurse. Whenever it got dry, Amran soaked it again and put it back on Ayaan's forehead. She cleaned Ayaan's upper body with another towel yet only let her hands and eyes go down as far as Ayaan's waist.

Despite her dazed and frenzied efforts to help Ayaan, eventually Amran noticed the shattered front door, flung wide open. She dashed to shut the back door and patched the smashed front one together, dragging all the living room items—couches and chairs—over to brace it up, beseeching God all along to save her sister and letting enough tears flow to fill a jar.

Ayaan closed her eyes and fell unconscious.

At last, dusk arrived and somewhere around eight o'clock, Ayaan's eyes opened on Amran staring at her like a guardian angel, or so she thought.

"Amran, my dear, are you well?" she whispered.

"I am well, darling," responded Amran. "How are you doing?"

"I am fine, dear." Her voice was feeble. "I feel as though the world has just been given back to me," she added.

"Oh, I'm so glad you're safe!" Amran cried. Waves of elation brought tears to her eyes, and then they spilled over. "Do you know where they took Cataaye?' she asked. "Will we ever see him again?"

When she saw Amran crying, Ayaan garnered the will to heave herself up. She leaned against the couch. The realization that her own life had been saved by her heroic little sister made her forget her own ordeal for a while. But joy did not last. Contemplating what she could say to Amran if her little sister asked Ayaan what had happened to her spoiled the moment.

But Amram never asked her older sister what had happened to her. The harshest question she conjured was to wonder what awful crime they could have committed against those people to deserve this.

Ayaan had no answer.

It took three days for Ayaan to pass beyond the immediate effect of her physical injuries and psychological trauma. She resumed her domestic duties, terrified that the vultures might come back and grieving over Caataye's unknown plight. She worried frantically over their food supplies, which were only enough to last them for another five days or so. She thought about how to make whatever food left last longer for her little sister.

Three days later, she decided against eating. She told Amran that she was fasting to make up for earlier Ramadan days she had missed. She let the little girl eat the scraps of what they had, stretching the days left.

But in four more days, their food had run out. On the fifth day, early in the morning, Ayaan was awakened by the revving of a car engine pulling into the driveway. With her heart palpitating and paralyzed by the terror of yet another ordeal, Ayaan shouted, "The vulture has landed, the vulture has landed!" After she had repeated the warning several times, it occurred to her that Amran was already in her hiding place, asleep. So she got out of her bed and ran into the living room.

By now someone was knocking on the door but in a civilized manner. Ayaan lifted the edge of the window curtain and saw a man in a regime's militia uniform. As he turned around,

Ayaan froze in horror. It was her Banaadir high school class-mate and secret admirer in Mogadishu from the days when the world seemed sane.

She had not seen Warsame since their graduation 12 years ago. Back then, they were both called *qaldaan* (she/he who is wrong), a teasing term used for northerners by their southerner classmates. She had neither known nor cared what tribe he belonged to, but now in this burdened era, she was suspicious that he might be kin to the man in power, who was responsible for the terror and destruction sweeping through the nation.

Yet Ayaan found she could not fear the man with the dreaded militia uniform. She sought solace in the fact that she had known Warsame when he was young. He was a brilliant, compassionate, and caring man, who fiercely protected her in high school. She also knew that though he was born in Lascaanood, he had gone to an elementary school in Berbera with her husband. They had become close friends and stayed friends long after, regardless of time and distance.

Remaining frozen at the window, she heard him whisper, "Ayaan, hurry up and open the door, please!"

Ayaan rushed from the window, dragged the couch and chairs out of the way, and let him in. Warsame extended his hand for a casual handshake, as the culture would have dictated in normal times, but this was far from a normal time. "Ayaan," he said, "how are you guys holding up?" But before she answered, he pulled her gently toward him, released her hand, and gave her a bear hug.

Ayaan threw herself softly on him, leaned on his shoulder, and wept. Warsame held her as she released her pain, letting tears trickle on his back. When she finally conjured up a bit of composure, Warsame freed one hand and, as Caataye had

done his last day with her, wiped her tears with his bare palm.
With his left hand still clinging to her waist, he maneuvered her
delicately onto the closest side of the couch and sat next to
her, freeing both of his hands.

"My sister Amran and I are still alive, Warsame," she finally
replied.

"Thank God for that, at least," Warsame sighed under his
breath, too soft for her to hear.

Though Ayaan had not heard him say it, she knew. The
sad look on his face said it all. She tried to keep herself from
asking but could not help.

"Warsame," she said, "is it as bad as I am thinking? Do you
know anything about him?"

Warsame's face darkened; but he dodged the bullet by
avoiding the question. "Ayaan," he said, "hurry up. Leave everything as it is and let us leave this carcass behind. Where
the hell is Amran anyway?"

When she heard the word carcass, Ayaan knew for sure
that he meant Caataye was no longer alive. But she still
wanted him to say the word. "Have you seen the body?" she
tried again, hoping to make it easier for Warsame.

But once again Warsame evaded the question. "Ayaan,"
he begged, "if we don't leave this place in a matter of minutes,
we will be lunch for those scavengers."

Realizing that she was not going to get him to tell the truth,
Ayaan shifted her efforts to rescue her sister. Without another
word, she dashed to Amran's hiding place and, in a matter of
seconds, was back, holding her by the hand. The two of them
tailgated Warsame, already racing toward his Land Rover,
parked outside.

Warsame opened the car door for them, pleading with them
to stay down low in the back seat, and drove off. The truck took

off at a mighty speed, zigzagging from one corner to another. Ayaan could tell that they were in downtown Hargeisa, but could not make out what direction they were heading. She had an urge to take a last look at the city in which she was born and raised, but for the sake of Warsame's pleading, as well as her little sister's safety, she did not dare.

Suddenly the car swerved to a screeching halt at the backyard of 26 June High School. Warsame jumped out and opened the left back door for Amran, grabbed her under the arms, put her gently on the ground, and signaled Ayaan to get out on the other side. Just as their feet touched the sand, an ambulance squealed to a halt beside them, just like Ayaan used to see in the movies long ago. In an instant three men jumped out, flung the back door open, and beckoned furiously for Ayaan, who, for her part, already had held up the hem of her gown in anticipation of leaping.

In another second, Ayaan and Amran were on the road. Ayaan could not help but glance at the two men in the regime's militia uniform who had positioned themselves behind the driver's seat. Both wore ammunition belts across their chests, kept their guns trained at the back of the ambulance, and displayed a look that declared to anyone ill-informed that they would kill for what they believed, if and when provoked by an enemy.

By now Ayaan guessed that they were westbound. But how to avoid the countless regime's militia check points, not to mention nearby Birjeex, the largest army base in the north? It worried her.

In fact, it immobilized her with terror. As they reached the first check point, the guards stormed the front door of the ambulance; fortunately, the head man recognized Warsame and suspended his impending harassment, which of course would have led only to more bloodshed had it gone on further.

Warsame, as it happened, was a commander of a special elite unit of the regime's army, called the Rescue Mission Force. His orders, which came directly from the Interior Minister, the dictator Barre's son-in-law, were to collect counter intelligence information even on officers loyal to the regime; for that reason, he was armed with presidential authority to go wherever he wished whenever he wished in the north. Warsame disguised his mission as an Emergency Transportation Unit, constantly in motion, connecting loose ends of every operation.

Actually, Warsame detested the demonic treatment meted out to the northern citizens, choosing to use his power to the fullest by veering away from the blind loyalty officer syndrome and rescuing as many women, children, and elderly as he could from the lion's jaws. He established well-placed connections with the rebel army, on the other side of the Ethiopian border, and amassed a reputation of being a moral man.

The guard who had come to Warsame's window gave a military salute and said, "Commander Warsame, how can we help you?"

It was just the music he was eager to hear. "Inform your commander that I am delivering blood supplies to a battalion at the front where supplies are running low. Tell him to send a telegram ahead, so that the checkpoints will not waste my time—and please, give him this letter." The letter Warsame handed over included a secret code for a presidential-level security clearance. He knew full well that their luck could vanish in seconds if they were exposed. As the guard ran with the message to his commanding officer, another opened the gate in haste, letting Warsame and his passengers through.

They had passed the first front peril. Warsame let out a

sigh of relief, and placed a careful look at one of the regime's army uniformed men, stationed now at the back of the ambulance for their protection. *He can't be more than 16-years-old,* he thought. Yet the young man's haggard face seemed to bear witness to several journeys through the valley of death and carried a warning to avoid him at all cost.

Since they had gotten into the ambulance, Warsame wanted to tell Ayaan that the driver and two fighters with him, despite the regime's army uniform, were all members of the guerrilla force fighting against the regime. But he remained silent lest he reveal more about their rescue operation.

Minutes later, Warsame watched Ayaan look to her left at the other man wearing the regime's army uniform. She was astonished and screamed, "Cilmi, I can't believe what my eyes are looking at or what my mind is telling me. Cilmi. Is that you?" The same man's rescue from Mandheera jail by the rebel force had sent shock-waves through Hargesia regime's Army Command. Ayaan rose from her seat, offering both hands.

He marveled how fast Cilmi stood up, extended his hands, held hers in his, released them, turned to Amran, pulled her up, and hugged her so tightly that they almost fell off the speeding car. He let her loose and, without a word, went back to his seat.

A few more times, the ambulance had to stop at checkpoints. Warsame brandished his secret presidential-level code but held his hand on his chest furtively each time, fearful his pounding heart muscles might force it open.

Five hours into their journey, the driver applied the brakes. Cilmi and the teenage guerrilla fighter stepped down from the back, Warsame and the driver from the front. Warsame walked to the back of the ambulance, held Amran by the arms, and helped lift her down. "If you want to stretch your legs, feel free," he said, "we are in Ethiopia now."

He thought Ayaan and Amran might not have had time to relieve themselves before leaving Hargeisa. This gave them the chance. A few minutes later, when the two sisters returned from their business in a nearby bush, Warsame and Cilmi were engaged in a heated discussion.

"What you are saying, Cilmi, is that the people we left behind in Hargesia are not suffering as well, so we can leave them there to die?" Warsame asked, sarcastic.

"No, that is not what I am saying at all. I am saying, now it's essential that you have to save your own life. And since you are not capable of doing so, I am obligated to save you from yourself."

"By the grace of God, I am going to be fine, thank you," Warsame asserted.

"Warsame, though God blinded the regime's army for the past two years, you know the sword of death has been hanging from a thread close to your neck. Our foes aren't fools; if they don't know about your rescue mission today, they will tomorrow. If you go back, you will probably never make it back, here or there."

Warsame and Cilmi were so absorbed in their quarrel, they had not noticed that Ayaan and Amran were standing beside them, hand in hand.

Warsame's eyes were wide with determination. "Cilmi," he said, "you know as well as I do that countless children are going to be orphaned, and countless mothers are going to be widowed."

Cilmi jumped in. "Warsame, which mother or father are you going to save next? When? Where and how?"

Warsame was not deterred. "I vow to fight for this just cause as long as I am alive."

"Fight," Cilmi shouted. "Warsame, let me refresh your memory, in case you've forgotten what fight means. It means you must be alive. After all, when I last checked, a dead body does not fight for its convictions, nor does it for the oppressed."

Now that Warsame's case was as clear to Ayaan as sunlight at noon, she raised her uninvited voice. "Warsame, if you go back to Hargeisa, I want you to know that I am going to go back with you."

Warsame looked at her. His mouth dropped open. Suddenly, his long-held secret came to the surface. *Perhaps all is not lost*, he thought. Maybe there was a glimmer of hope that if they would make it out, all safe, there could still be room to start over. Gazing back and forth between Ayaan and Amran, Cilmi standing next to them and the two guerilla fighters engaged 20 feet away, he stood there, motionless.

As they all waited for him to do or say something, the only sound they could hear, like a dissonant violin, was the wind's vibration beating on trees.

As he stood there, he heard Amran plead, "Warsame, please, don't take us back to Hargeisa to die."

His eyes were already red. Now he bit his lower lip as he motioned Ayaan to loosen her clutch on Amran. Then he stood between the two sisters. With one hand on Ayaan's arms and the other on Amran's, he turned around. In union, they walked west, where the ambulance was ready bound for Ethiopia, waiting.

Cilmi, grinning from ear to ear, rushed to join them. The driver and the two guerilla fighters clapped loudly for the four friends, marching on in celebration of survival.

A Delicate Hope

Translated from Somali by Ahmed Ismail Yusuf and Fred Pfeil

Ever since word arrived from the Saudi Embassy that a letter was going to be hand delivered to him in a matter of days, Aar had chosen to imprison himself in the house where he was raised. It was consoling, of course, that the diabolically corrupt government of Mogadishu would have no knowledge of the letter and no way to intercept it. On the other hand, the message was so ambiguous that there was no way to tell when it was best to wait. So Aar came up with an idea of his own, which he called an "Ambition Imprisonment," for he decided to wait for the letter, day and night, in his home.

His identical twin Arbaab offered to give him a hand. In more normal times, Arbaab would have amused Aar with his sarcastic humor. But these days, Arbaab himself was very tight on time, given the fact that he was attending the National University of Lafoole (the best in the nation), double majoring in math and physics. Yet still when they got together, they would argue about anything and nothing in particular. Whenever Arbaab, a skillful debater, attacked social science or literary arts, Aar felt vulnerable. He had been a psychology major and had also managed to publish several short stories in his late teenage years. He was artistic and versed in poetry and prose, but not analytical in science like his brother.

This afternoon, when Arbaab arrived home from college for the weekend, he placed his bag on the living room sofa and greeted everyone. Before his shower, he found his brother.

Aar was sitting at the front door steps. Arbaab sat next to him. "Aar," he said, looking right into his brother's eyes, "I bet that messenger you have been waiting for is a psychologist. If so, I can tell you what's happened to him, but you have to be man enough to ask."

"Oh, man. Not again, Arbaab. Please don't give me your baloney. I can't hear it now, OK?"

"So, what you're telling me is that you aren't going to stand up for your colleagues," Arbaab said.

"If I ask what, that would be the wrong question since I know you will carry on and on," said Aar. "Then God knows when and where it's going to end."

"Tell you what. Whether you're going to listen or not, I am going to say it but I am going to be fair-minded at least; I promise you that. That letter of yours was trusted to a young psychologist just out of a graduate school. But before I go on, I have to say one good thing about him. He is very ambitious and thinks illnesses of the entire human race can be cured by psychotherapy. Anyway, he flew from Dahran, Saudi Arabia. En-route to Mogadishu, the airplane stopped in Nairobi. During the flight to Nairobi, he met this charming mother of nine from Kenya who was going through a painful divorce. She told him that she had been married to the same man for 10 years. You don't have to understand advanced calculus to figure out that she must have been having a child every year. So just to have a conversation, she confided her secret to this stranger, knowing that she wasn't going to see him again. What a better way to relieve herself, right? He was not going to talk about her to anybody she knew..."

"Does this nonsense end anytime soon?" Aar interrupted.

"Just when I was about to climax, you interrupted; of course, it has an end. Again, I was on the verge of getting to the juicy part. Patience, patience is a virtue, my friend."

"It looks to me like the judgment day will be here before you get there," Aar said.

"All right," Arbaan sighed. "I hear that you are a bit on edge. So let me make the long story short."

"Please do," Aar said, "though I could care less about it either way."

"If I may proceed, please, sir."

"Yeah, yeah, go on, Mister Genius," said Aar.

"That is very kind of you, sir. Thanks. Now, where was I?" asked Abaab.

Aar looked at the sky and said, "Oh, God. You want me to wait for the end of a story and you don't know where you left off."

"Relax, brother, and loosen up a little. We are coming to the fun part. Now, when the young psychologist heard the poor lady's heartbroken story, he insisted that she had to clear her mind by pouring the venomous grief in her soul and heart out to him. There on the airplane, he started a marathon psychotherapy session. By the time the airplane landed in Nairobi, one tape was already filled and another just started. Realizing that they were nowhere near the end, he offered to continue the session on land. There, he got off the airplane in Nairobi and followed the woman home with your letter in his pocket. That is where your letter lies, waiting to be rescued."

Aar waved his hands in the air, looked down at his feet. "Dear God, please forgive my brother whose idea of commiseration lacks the human touch."

At that same moment, their mother came out of the house and sat one step down from the two brothers. "Wait, wait a minute, Arbaab," she said. "What if the messenger was a young poet or writer? Wouldn't you think he would hurry to deliver the message if only to share with a fellow writer his passion for words?"

"Aw, Mom, that is even worse. Ask me why," Arbaab said as Aar rolled his eyes and shook his head.

"Why?" his mother asked.

"On his way to Mogadishu, a fellow Egyptian poet offered him a gift of a newly printed never-before-published book of Omar Khayyam's poems. The young poet immersed himself in the verses, and then unwittingly got off the plane in Nairobi. Now, there is no way to tell when he will realize that he had made a mistake and catch the next flight to Mogadishu, provided he is at least conscientious enough to know that Africa is a continent and Somalia isn't Kenya and Kenya isn't Somalia."

Whenever the two brothers dragged their mother into their conversation, she would offer her opinion but ended up only proving to herself that she was not able to match a tenacious teenage debate. She stood up and said, "You two settle it yourselves," and went back to the house.

The brothers were so involved in their playful argument that they hardly noticed she was gone.

"Mr. Quantum Theory," Aar said, "as your always gracious brother, I have to remind you once more that your high school geography is failing you. Why would a sane person take off from Saudi Arabia and fly over Somalia to Kenya when his final destination is Somalia?"

"See, Aar, you have once again failed to see the light of wisdom. You fellows in psychology have total disregard for the factors of cost and distance."

"OK, OK, but what does that deficiency of ours have to do with the topic at hand?"

"Because," said Arbaab, "it's Economics 101. An airplane carrying passengers to Kenya would drop them off first in

Kenya rather than stopping first at Mogadishu, taking off for Nairobi, and then coming back to Mogadishu again empty."

"I am not going to win regardless, so I might as well shut my mouth," said Aar.

"Aar, I figured I'd just tease you a little to make sure that your old spirit is still here," said Arbaab and nudged his brother with his shoulder. "But you are turning into a prisoner of solitary confinement. The only difference is that yours is voluntary. Let me offer you a deal, brother: from now on, every Thursday afternoon and all Friday, I will be here waiting for your letter. So please go try to have a bit of fun with the girls or at least gossip about them."

"Come on, Arbaab," Aar said. "In all honesty, do you think that when Asha, Hibo, or Anisa calls or stops by, you'll remember why you've promised to stay home?"

Arbaab smiled. "Yes, when it comes to women, I am prone to disavow my loyalty to men, including my own twin brother. But in all seriousness, let me ask you this: What can I do to share some of the burden with you?"

"Arbaab, listen. Have as much sex as you can for both of us but please, don't mention my name."

"I'm not going to win this, am I?"

"No," Aar said. "Not this time. I am just trying to nurse a hope, a very delicate hope!"

"I'd better hit the shower then," said Arbaab. He stood up, dusted off his pants, and went in.

Aar's delicate hope had begun to bloom a few months ago at King Saud University, when a prominent faculty member and Saudi writer, Dr. Qasim, had come across one of Aar's published short stories. He had seen Aar's name in a magazine and at first thought it was a former student of his. By the time he got to the middle of the story, however, he knew that he had never seen this writing style before. He turned the pages back to take another look at the writer's name and biography. It wasn't anybody he knew, but the short story intrigued him enough to make him look around for more work by this distinctive young writer. After reading the few other stories he could get his hands on, Dr. Qasim found himself writing to this young man he had never met. In his letter, he asked if Aar had more stories, and what he could do for him that might enhance the prospect of sharing his writing with a wider audience.

"Such a talent as yours, especially in a young man for whom Arabic is not his native tongue, is an inspiration to us," Dr. Qasim wrote. "I am positive that Arabic language scholars who come to know your art will cheer your craft. Would you please be kind enough to enlist me as your friend? And likewise, please do not hesitate to let me know if there is anything humanly possible that I could do to enhance the opportunity to share your writing with better judges than myself."

Aar was numb for quite some time. He could not believe that a Saudi writer and faculty member had not only taken an interest in his stories, but also responded by writing to him.

Aar soon called his brother on the phone and recited the letter, word for word. Once they were done shouting for joy, they agreed that if Aar could secure a residential visa plus a full scholarship with the accompanying generous allowance from the Saudi government, then he would manage to find a way out of Mogadishu to India for both Arbaab and their mother. They decided to tell their mother only that a prominent King Saud University faculty member had read Aar's short stories and liked them well enough to respond, so she wouldn't be too disappointed if the whole thing fell through.

Aar didn't waste a minute. "Dear Dr. Qasim," he wrote.

"Your letter has found me. It has lifted my spirit, lit up my house of hope, and elevated my pride. I would like to thank you for the time you took to read my stories and for your kind words, which you showered upon my work. You have no idea how much these words from a prominent writer and scholar like you mean to me. I hardly have words to explain but can only say that your letter has been inspirational and encouraging. I never thought this miracle could happen to me, yet you have proven me wrong. What a surprise!

"Finally, I hope that you will not mind if I take you up on your kind offer to give me some assistance, since I would like to request admission into your University. I am sending you my transcript along with some other negligible work of mine, both published and unpublished. Please evaluate them all as one, and let me know whether or not I am worthy of your University's excellent instruction."

Aar did not say what was really on his mind. He did not let on that he was wandering the streets of Mogadishu, that he had been expelled from the National University of Lafoole when he refused to spy on his fellow students for the National Secret Service. It was his nature to avoid politics in general, yet he had fallen victim to the severity of injustice in his motherland.

So, as the days passed, Aar wondered whether Dr. Qasim was for real, and if he were, whether the letter had reached him, and if it had, whether he still cared about it enough to respond. And if by a miracle of God he responded, whether it would arrive in Aar's hand safely.

A month later, at 7:00 at night, someone knocked on the door. When Aar's mother opened it, she found a tall, white, Arabian-looking man standing on the doorsteps. As he tried to greet her, she flinched and almost slammed the door on his face but caught herself.

"I am sorry," she said in Arabic. "I guess I was expecting a Somali face. What can I do for you?"

"Is Aar in?" the Arab asked.

The mother was consumed with fear. She had no idea who this man standing in front of her was. She had not heard Aar mention any foreign friends. Frantically, but without success, she searched for reasons why a stranger would ask for Aar. "Ah, um, eeh, no," she said. "He isn't . . . he isn't in the house."

The stranger let out what seemed to her a million words in Arabic that she, with her meager hoard of the Arabic language, couldn't possibly keep up with. As the mother stood there staring, though, it must have occurred to him that she did not know enough of the language to give him a satisfactory answer. He turned his back on her and walked toward his American Cadillac with a diplomatic license plate while the mother looked on apprehensively.

"Anyone can have any license plate they wish these days," she whispered to herself. After all, it wasn't every day an Arab man would come to her door, asking for her son. Was government security masquerading as an Arab in order to come here to arrest her child? If so, what was the reason?

But she knew, of course, that there didn't have to be any reason at all. While the twins were in high spirits most of the time, their mother didn't share their lighthearted mood. She was gravely concerned about what the days ahead might hold for her adored sons, and anxious about her status in a society that had no place for a poor, divorced, middle-aged mother. The dark blanket of corruption that covered her nation and the senseless human slaughter the so-called government had waged against the northern people (and would no doubt unleash here in the south) gnawed constantly at her mind. Though she had dreamed of watching her twins bloom, go to college, marry and have their own children, lately her main goal had become simply their survival, nothing more than that.

Now, however, just before the man vanished into his car, Aar, always on guard, came out of his room and quickly asked his mother who had rung the doorbell.

Fortunately, as she began telling him about the Arab man who had just been there looking for him, he saw the man through the window, getting into his car.

Aar dashed out of the house screaming, "I am Aar, I am Aar," and caught the man half in and half out of his car.

The man stopped, got out, turned around, and leaned against his car. "Are you hiding from Barre?" he said in a sarcastic tone.

Surprised that an Arab diplomat would be so bold as to say something about the repressive regime whose sovereignty his own government had pledged to uphold, Aar said, "My mother is overly cautious. Please excuse her uncharitable behavior."

"Well, I have been in Somalia long enough to know that isn't so odd. Who would blame her?" said the Arab man. "Oh, please forgive me for not introducing myself to you." He held out his hand. "*Asalaama calaykum*, my brother. My name is Faruq Essah, from the Saudi Embassy. Call me Faruq."

"*Wa calakum masalaam*, my brother. My name is Aar Saeed, please call me Aar." Aar approached and extended his hand.

"Aar, let me tell you why I am here," said Faruq as they shook hands. "I have a message from Dr. Qasim for you. You know, of course, that in my country he is a national treasure, an expert on the Islamic world, and a brilliant scholar of the Arabic language. He is now, however, quite concerned about Somalia and wants to help as best he can."

As he spoke, Faruq gradually straightened up from where he had been leaning against his car. Standing fully erect, he pulled out a telegram from his pocket. "Hold on, hold on," he said. "I am awfully sorry, I should have given you this telegram first."

"No, no, that's OK," responded Aar as he took the telegram and unfolded it with trembling hands.

"My dear brother, Aar," the letter read, "King Saud University is glad to have you as a student and happy to be able to provide you a scholarship. We feel privileged to offer you the guidance that you have asked of us. The details of this scholarship will be fully explained to you by my young friend Faruq, who has agreed to be emissary for this matter. Soon after you have met him, we will send you a package including a visa. Like this telegram, however, any messages passing between us will be hand delivered. *Insha'Allah*, you will hear from us shortly. Until then, stay calm and keep praying."

When Aar finished reading, he folded the telegram and clutched it in his hand so tightly that it hurt. Tears formed in his eyes, and in humility he surrendered himself to the total gratitude he felt. He searched for words but could not find them. He tried to constrain the tears and calm himself, but he couldn't. Finally he muttered, "I, I, I don't know what to say, Faruq. At this moment, it is all too much for me."

"You don't have to say anything, Aar. From what I have heard, you deserve it. Now let us work on the rest. First, let me explain a little bit about your scholarship. Housing will be provided for you. Are you married?"

"No, at least not yet," Aar replied.

"Is there a marriage on the way in the coming days?" Faruq asked.

"Oh, no, no," Aar laughed. "I only meant, *insha'Allah*, maybe one day but not now, nor in the days ahead."

"I only asked because if you were, we have to make housing arrangements accordingly. Anyway, as I was saying, the housing is provided, the tuition is paid, and an allowance of $1500 per month is paid to you by the government. The other news that I would like you to hear is that the Saudi Embassy, like the rest of the world, has decided to pull its staff out of Mogadishu. But don't despair. I am going to stay behind with the Egyptian Embassy, which has decided against pulling out, long enough to ensure your departure. Aar, I have to leave now, but remember—you are going to hear from us in person. Expect me to show up at any moment, for I will be back again as soon as your package arrives from Saudi Arabia. Until then, so long, friend. I leave you in the hands of Almighty God."

They shook hands, bade each other farewell, and Faruq disappeared into his car and drove off into the streets of Mogadishu, leaving Aar to take the few steps back to his front door, wobbling under the weight of joy. As he sat on his doorstep, his thoughts traveled through galaxies unknown to men, begging heaven's angels to explain why he had been so blessed.

Eventually, alarmed at her son's motionlessness, his mother came out of the house, calling his name. When he didn't respond, she sat beside him, put her hand on his shoulder, and asked a thousand questions. "Aar, what happened? Who was that man? What did he say? Oh God, is Arbaab OK?"

Finally, when Aar still didn't answer, she resorted to the natural relief of tears. Only then did Aar come back to mother earth. He hugged his mother and began recapping the news to her.

"Hooyo," he said. "Remember the King Saud University faculty member I told you about, the one who read my stories?"

"Yes," she said.

"Well, I didn't tell you the whole story. I wrote to him and now he has written me back. I asked him for admission to the University, and the upshot is that they granted me not only admission but a full scholarship too. Mom, I have a telegram stating all the facts. That man you spoke with was from the Saudi Embassy, and he explained everything about the scholarship to me. But I have not even begun to tell you where you and Arbaab come into all of this."

"Son," she interrupted, "we are already part of anything that concerns you."

"Yes, Mom," Aar said, "but this is very special. There is a $1500 per month allowance that I am not going to need since the housing, books, and tuition are all paid. That means you and Arbaab are going to be able to get out of here, too. With that kind of money, in fact, Arbaab can go to any school he wants to in India, and there will be more than enough left over for you to live the life you're entitled to. There is only one catch."

"And what is that?" she asked.

"I have to wait a few days for the visa and scholarship package," he said, "but no one knows when it will arrive."

"Perhaps it isn't so wise to pin your hopes on a promissory note," his mother warned.

"Maybe so, Mom," Aar said, grinning from ear to ear. "But you know I am a sucker for optimism and live off my high hopes."

"Now," he proceeded, "I have to imprison myself in the house to wait for this package since my entire future and the future of my family depends on it. The man told me that the package will be hand delivered to me but there is no definite time to expect it. So I am going to be here 24 hours a day, seven days a week—tomorrow, the day after tomorrow, and the day after that. Mom, the farthest I will go will be right here on our front doorsteps. Ambition Imprisonment it is—yes, that's exactly what it is. Ambition Imprisonment."

His mother could not share his confidence—not after learning about the uncertainty of the waiting involved. But she was not about to let her doubts and fears puncture his pouch of hope. "*Insha'Allah*," she said, "it will all come true for you." She went into the house, leaving him there, waiting.

Three weeks later, at 10 at night, the doorbell's ring rippled three times through the house. Since it was raining, Aar did not expect it to be his messenger. But his vigilant mind impelled him to rush for the door. There was Faruq, standing in the doorway, anxious to be let in. The Islamic greeting rituals ensued and he was quickly let into the house.

"Listen," he said, "I have everything in hand—the visa, the ticket, the scholarship package, and the information that goes along with it. I've also got the stamper to validate your visa, so please get your passport out."

Aar dashed into his room and returned with the passport. Faruq plugged in the stamper and applied it to the passport. "There," he said, "you're all set to sail. But there's just one more thing."

"What?" Aar asked.

"The Saudi airline is going to suspend its service in Somalia indefinitely. The last flight leaves tomorrow afternoon at 4:00 p.m. Please, whatever you do, be there! *Insha'Allah*, Aar, you will make it."

Again they bade each other a hasty farewell, and Faruq left the house as quickly and silently as he had come. Aar closed the door behind him and, a moment later, slowly lowered himself to the carpet to sit and think. This should have been the moment for a victory dance but he was in no mood for celebration. The worst civil war ever in his country was fast approaching from the north, where Isaaq, a tribal-based rebel group, had seized control of the devastated cities, mined wells, and scorched farmland that the regime's militia had left behind in their retreat. Now that the fighting was only miles away from the capital Mogadishu, Barre's army desperately needed manpower to turn the tide, so it was conscripting any man who could lift a gun. Even now, sporadic gunfire erupted in the city streets every so often, and the BBC, the Voice of America, and other international radio stations were carrying the news of foreign embassies' emergency evacuations.

Aar sat in the middle of the living room, riffling through the pages of his scholarship booklet. Everything was there, just as he'd been told. Yet all he could do was sit and stare at the words.

A few minutes later, his mother came out of the kitchen, wiping her hands on a towel, and found her son sitting in a silent heap on the floor. Her hands stopped moving; her mind became still with alarm. "What is it, my son?" she asked.

When Aar showed her the package and restated what Faruq had told him about the urgency of his departure, she forced her mind to focus, and took heart. "Well, my son, we don't have much time to waste. Let us get to it and weigh every available option."

They started with the vexing problem of how to reach the airport the next day, knowing full well that Aar would be sent to fight against his own people if the military got hold of him on his way there. Finally, after frustrating, fruitless hours, Aar stood up and walked in a circle in the living room. The thought of calling Arbaab occurred to him but then he looked at the clock and realized it was almost midnight. In the next instant, though, the ringing of the phone broke the silence. Frantically, Aar rushed over and picked up the receiver.

"Hello?"

"How are you doing, guys?" said a cheerful voice on the other end.

"Oh, thank God, Arbaab. I was going to call you, but then I thought of how late it is and those killer Saturday classes of yours."

"Actually," Arbaab said, "I had gone to bed earlier but something woke me up, and then I had this urge to call. You know how it is, Aar. The 'telepathic twins' thing, I guess! So, what's up with you and Mom?"

"We are both fine," said Aar, "but my scholarship package and the visa arrived this evening. I have to get to the airport and catch the last flight of Saudi Airline at four o'clock. You know what the situation is like. How I am going to . . . ?"

"4:00 this morning?" Arbaab interrupted.

"No, no, 4:00 in the afternoon. But how I am going to get to the airport, let alone secure a seat on that flight?"

"You almost gave me a heart attack for a moment there, buddy. Relax, Aar, please," said Arbaab. "We have plenty of time and I assure you, we will have a plan by then."

"Arbaab," Aar sighed, "all this bloodshed, the conscription, foreigners' evacuations . . . They are taking a toll on me."

"I know, brother, I know," Arbaab said. "But we have to beat it, and we will. We will beat it, you'll see. Tell you what," he continued, "here's a plan. Tomorrow you get dressed up like a religious woman, call a cab, and sit in the back. That'll give the impression that a sister with veil is sitting in the back seat, avoiding close proximity with the driver, so no one will bother you. Then, when you get to the airport, change back to your regular clothes before you get out of the cab."

"That may not be bad, but do you really think it'll work?"

"Why not? It must work, and it will," said Arbaab. "Besides, we have no alternatives, nor do we have the luxury of time."

"OK, OK, Arbaab. I will do just that. But I guess that means I won't get to see you then. Because I beg you, don't even think about coming to the airport. Do you hear me, Arbaab? Please, Arbaab. Please."

Silence on the other end of the phone lingered a bit, then softly Arbaab said, "Sure, Brother. I will not. I will not come to the airport."

"And promise that you'll take care of Mom for me."

"Of course, I will," Arbaab murmured.

"I'll send for you as soon as I get situated there."

"I'm sure you will, Brother," Arbaab said.

"Goodbye for now, Brother," said Aar, choking out the words.

"Goodbye, Aar," said Arbaab. He sounded like he was barely holding the tears back himself.

As soon as Aar and his mother woke up the next morning, they embarked on the next step of securing transportation to the airport. They agreed that the mother would go out to hire a reliable cab to pick up Aar an hour and a half before the airplane's departure. As agreed upon, Aar's mother ventured out and fortunately ran into a young man whose family she had known. She promised five times more than the regular fare to the airport, sealed the deal with him, and came back home.

By noon of that fateful day, Aar's mother was trying out women's religious garb on him, together with the latest facial adornment, just in case anyone might peep through the veil. She did so well that when Aar looked at himself in the mirror, he was shocked and a bit embarrassed to see his feminine side staring back at him.

At 2:30 p.m., the cabdriver blew the horn. Prior to the taxi's arrival, mother and son had agreed to take leave of each other at home, and for Aar to get word of his departure to her through a friend of his who worked for the Saudi airline in Dahran.

Tearfully, mother and son kissed each other goodbye for the first time in 21 years. A moment later, a young, proper Muslim woman slid into the back seat of the cab, with only a single small package and purse as "her" luggage. Aar waved goodbye to his mother one more time as the driver pulled away from the house.

The driver sped west, weaving through Mogadishu's streets, and reached the airport gate unmolested. Quickly, Aar shed his shell, put his shirt and pants back on, got out and took off to get in line. Before reaching the ticket counter, Aar's progress was arrested by a melee of people roaming around like mad cows in their desperate attempts to reach the same destination. Swallowed up in the chaotic wave, he managed to learn that the damnable Duub Cas, an especially oppressive unit of the military police that also served as dictator Barre's bodyguards, were holding the crowd back, with orders to shoot to kill all those who would break through the line. So people kept stampeding back onto each other every time one of the ghoulish soldiers turned towards them.

In a few minutes, Aar learned that the Saudi airline itself had been given an ultimatum: take Barre's relatives and immediate family out of the country or else ground its planes altogether. Now reality was staring back at him with naked eyes.

His hope to board the airplane was hanging from a thread. And then the thread snapped.

At 4:30 p.m., from within the roiling crowd, he was able to

see the Saudi airplane taxi down the runway and lift off into the air. Too distraught even to feel despair, he walked out of the airport, oblivious to all that was around, got into the first cab he saw, and called out his home address in a hollow voice.

A mile or so away from the airport, Aar realized that the cabdriver had just made a wrong turn. Trembling with a sudden, overwhelming rage, he yelled at the driver to turn back and take the right road. But instead of complying, the pseudo cabdriver pulled out a pistol and badge. "Welcome to the army," he announced with a grin. "You are now a proud member of the infantry, Division 21st October."

"Thank you, Sir," Aar said. "Well, well, well. What a surprise! Aren't we all proud of shedding brethren blood, or shall I dare say fratricide, just for the heck of a fancy word?"

The officer-cabdriver swerved to the curb and yelled, "If you say that again—one more time—I am going to empty this barrel on your fucking head. Do you understand that, you bastard?"

"Go ahead, why don't you?" Aar shouted back. "Go ahead and prove to yourself what a worthy authority figure you are. I am sure that will make you a hero."

The militia officer double-checked the security locks on the car and got out. The man he had captured was clearly a loose cannon, so loose that he did not trust himself, alone and unaided, to drive him to the camp. So he called on his walkie-talkie for backup, which soon arrived and transferred Aar to the back of a prisoner's truck. It rolled away, destination unknown.

Over the next two weeks in training camp, Aar feigned fervent loyalty successfully enough to be allowed to join a special Intelligence Unit. He did it to avoid the battlefield and the risk of having to kill another mother or child. Meantime, through frantic effort, his mother managed to locate Aar's friend in Saudi Arabia and learned that he had not been on the passenger list of the last Saudi plane out. Not long after, the National University of Lafoole suspended all classes indefinitely, since half of the student body had been taken off to mysterious camps somewhere outside of the capital.

For Aar's family, the only bright spot in this world of woes was that Arbaab had made it home from the University without being nabbed as well.

Then, one uneventful day, two months after Aar had disappeared, Arbaab and his mother received a letter from him, his passport enclosed. Aar's letter told them that he had been conscripted by the so-called national army but they must be patient and take care of his passport. Soon, he would get a chance to escape.

Just knowing that Aar was still alive warmed his mother's heart and sent his brother's soul to seventh heaven. Though his mother was skeptical of his chances of safe escape, she wanted, impatiently, to move on to the next hurdle.

"Arbaab," the mother called out, "of course we are ecstatic that he is alive and well, but we have to get to the next stage of planning a getaway to the north as soon as he arrives, if he ever makes it, that is. And before my sons leave for the north, you have to know your maternal clan affiliation and my ancestors' names, to use them if need be, all by heart."

"Mom," Arbaab pleaded. "What in the world is in the north for us? Over and over you keep insisting that we have to know the names of a bunch of ancestors who've been dead for centuries. Mom, I know you're from the northern clan of Isaaq and I know my father is Darood, also from the north. I will never affiliate myself with either one if I can't belong to both. And you know Aar and I are in the same boat on this. If we are going to die anyhow, Mom, for an unjust tribal war, let us not sow a poison seed for the generations to come by choosing one tribe over the other."

Pondering the power of his sermon, the mother retired into heart-wrenching tears. Yet she was unable to let go of her point once and for all. Hours later, they had agreed that their only choice was to escape to the north for the time being, but the question of the tribal allegiance remained unsettled.

"As far as I am concerned," the mother persisted, "Isaaq is your maternal clan, and so they will not harm you . . . ."

"Mom," Arbaab interrupted, "you're at it again! Please let's not go down that road, all right?"

"OK, OK," she sighed. "Then what different escape plan do you have in mind?"

Arbaab was silent for a moment, and then he threw his arms up. "I don't have a clue, Mom, not a clue."

"I know someone who used to travel around with his donkey wagon, selling hay off the back of it. But now he transports human cargo along with the hay. He takes two or three passengers at a time, covers them with hay, reaches a rendezvous point, and then off to the north they go. The militia never searches the wagon since they think all it's carrying is insignificant, just heaps of hay."

"Wow, that is it, Mom. That is it!" said Arbaab. "Now all we have to do is find the guy."

They agreed that she would go out looking for the hay seller. When she found him the very next day, he agreed to pick up her sons when and where she said, and assured her that the operation was virtually risk free. Their plan was sealed.

Days dragged on and turned into weeks, and then months. But one bright day, a shabbily dressed man with a wild scraggy beard and a twisted, flimsy cane came to the window and knocked. Arbaab angrily signaled for him to go away but the beggar would pay no heed. Finally, Arbaab opened the front door to tell him they had nothing to offer so he might as well move on. There was something in the beggar's faint smile, however, that seemed vaguely familiar so Arbaab leaned forward on the doorstep to get a closer look. At that point, the beggar could no longer hold his muffled laughter in. Arbaab was forced to open his trembling arms to embrace the stranger before he realized, all at once, that the gaunt, ragged beggar in his arms was his brother. A second later their mother, awakened by their howls of joy, come out to the front room and joined her cries with theirs.

Within a few minutes, the three of them, still holding tightly to one another, were sitting side by side in the living room where they let questions and replies fly free. Arbaab could not get over the brilliance of Aar's disguise, which seemed equal to anything the infamous CIA and its counterpart, the KGB of many years past, could have concocted. Then Aar took the reins and talked awhile about what seemed to him just a mere fraction of his odyssey but to his mother and brother sounded like the tales in *The Thousand and One Nights*. He told them how he had stashed his passport and the scholarship package in a bathroom in the first camp he had been sent to, and boasted gleefully of having fooled the militia into trusting him as a trained intelligence officer. He described how he had planned and hatched his own escape. His account was only interrupted by trips to the bathroom and bites of the food his mother cooked, running back and forth to the kitchen, making sure he had enough. Before any of them noticed, the clock on the wall pointed to well after midnight, so they had to adjourn.

Ironically, throughout this chronicle of his adventures in hell, Aar showed no sign of fatigue. The next day, though, when

Arbaab and his mother woke up, Aar remained motionless in his bed. The only sign of life was his breathing. So Arbaab and the mother moved on to plan the departure to the north without his input, concluding that it was best for Aar to have a whole day of rest before taking the trip early the next morning. When Aar finally woke up that afternoon, they told him about the arrangements. The two brothers were to take the trip; their mother would stay behind in hopes of joining them later. Knowing that the risk of staying in Mogadishu increased with every minute, Aar had no choice but to agree to their plan.

Once again, the mother went out to the streets to find the hay seller and tell him that it was time. The two of them agreed that he would pick the brothers up the next morning at 4:00. Sure enough, at 4:00 a.m., the hay seller arrived. This time, all eyes were dry as Aar and Arbaab bade their mother goodbye, jumped on board, and took refuge in the thick pile of hay. At several checkpoints on the road, they came very close to the dreaded militia on guard. Fortunately, though, no one took any interest in a donkey wagon full of hay.

Finally, many miles away, the wagon came to a halt. The hay seller put his fingers in his mouth, letting out a sharp, piercing whistle. In no time, a beat-up jeep with two girl passengers and a male driver came into view. Before the jeep came to a stop, the hay seller shouted to Aar and Arbaab to get off and board the car. The next thing they knew, they were on the highway to the north.

By noon, the car was passing by Beled Weyn. Aar pinched his brother and beckoned to the sky. It was a brilliantly clear and sunny day in the middle of an exceptionally harsh and prolonged winter. The trees were naked and the land was dry.

The sand was a reddish dust, disturbed here and there by dead animals lying along the side of the road. Yet to the right of them, perhaps a quarter of a mile away, half a dozen hawks were diving, one after the other, down from the open sky, zeroing in on two rabbits, which collided with each other in their desperate flight for their lives. On their left, hundreds of migrating geese flew next to their speeding car as though in a losing race with it, until the distance between them grew so great that they were swallowed up by the horizon's haze.

Hours upon hours later, approaching the outskirts of the liberated city of Burco, Aar and Arbaab felt no fear when their car was brought to a halt by soldiers of the rebel army controlling the region. Feeling no allegiance to either their paternal or maternal clan, they wanted to be part of the emancipated city instead, and saw the entire northern dissenters as "liberators," whose resistance to human degradation offered an indelible lesson for all oppressed men around the world.

The "liberators" ordered everyone out of the car and instructed them to identify themselves. To Aar and Arbaab's utter dismay, the women not only told their clan and subclan but recited a list of their forefathers' names in reverse order, the same way their mother had tried to teach them, but to no avail. The driver followed and did the same, and the three of them were quickly released, hassle free.

Now, quite clearly, it was up to Aar and Arbaab to do the same. But the two could go no further than stating their names and their father's name. They were quick to protest that although they had been born in Mogadishu, their father and mother both had come from the north. But as they realized that what they were saying wasn't what the crazed guards waited to hear, the enormity of their mistake sank in. Frantically, they babbled what little they knew about the clan identity that they despised. But they knew full well that the little information they could provide failed to verify the subclan connection of either of their parents. And their unconventional twins' names—Aar, the male lion, and Arbaab, the male elephant—only added fuel to the fire.

The head of the guards, a man about the same age as Aar, was not amused. "You, Aar, are a lion," he bellowed, "so you are supposed be a terror to Isaaq. And since you, Arbaab, are an elephant, you are supposed to march on us, just as freely as the elephant saunters across open land."

The suspicion that the young brothers were spies for Barre's regime hung thickly in the air. They were arrested for espionage. The guards dragged them into a shanty jail and told them that their fate would be decided within 30 minutes— by a kangaroo court composed of the jailors themselves.

Then the final blow fell on their heads. A man who had escaped from the same battalion of Barre's army from which Aar had fled recognized him and quickly confided this piece of information to his rebel colleagues. A minute later, the brothers were told they had been found guilty, and that the penalty for their crime was death. As spies and traitors to the nation, the two of them were not deemed worthy of bullets.

As they were led in shackles out of the jail and toward the gallows, Aar made one last valiant effort to save his brother. "Do whatever you wish with me!" he cried out. "But know that my brother Arbaab has never, never served in the military!"

As Aar pleaded with his captors not to spill any more innocent blood on land already saturated with it, Arbaab plodded along in silence broken only by the grating of his chains. By the time they reached the gallows, Aar's voice was no longer audible, yet his mouth remained open as though he were gasping for air.

Beneath the menacing square of the gibbet, they were brought to a halt and, in the same instant, felt the rope from above descending to rest softly on their shoulders. The executioners tightened the nooses around their necks and hoisted them up like two flimsy flags.

Before the corpses were lowered to the ground, a senior commander stopped by to check on his guards. Taking in what had just happened, he requested a briefing. The guard in charge went on and on about where the two boys came from and what they had been accused of but it was some time before he finally referred to their names.

The commander could not believe his ears. Three more times, he made the guard repeat himself before walking over from his Land Rover to examine the bodies now lying on the ground. He turned the bodies over, one by one, and then drew back from them, writhing like a man in flames. "Aar and Arbaab," he wailed. "My flesh and blood . . . they were my nephews, they were my nephews, my nephews . . . ."

Insane and consumed with grief, he turned around and opened fire with his AK-47 on the guards, killing five and wounding four before running out of bullets. Then, out of his sidearm holster, he pulled a pistol and shot himself.

The Lion's Binding Oath

Hassan was in a math class at Jamal Abdinasir High School in Mogadishu in 1990 when RPG firearms began to crackle in the distance. Most of his classmates pretended to ignore it but Hassan wondered whether a rebel army that his mother had been talking about had arrived from the north. In minutes, the sound intensified and grew closer and closer.

Suddenly from the next room came another teacher who whispered something to his teacher. As though in agreement, Hassan's teacher nodded and watched the other leave, closing the door behind him. His teacher leaned back on the board, paused, looked down, lifted his gaze and said, "We aren't exactly sure what is going on out there but I suggest that we call it a day. Go home, guys, and please be careful."

Students rushed out of the class and onto the streets but Hassan lingered a bit longer. He wondered what his teacher was being told. And why didn't he share it with the class? Now that everybody was out though, Hassan decided to do the same. About a mile from home, he watched smoke rise here and there from the northeast, drifting west. It occurred to him that the RPG firearms were crackling louder, spreading east. He was running now as fast as he could but the distance between his school and house seemed to increase.

Panting and out of breath, he made it to the gate of his house. Once inside, his mother and two of his sisters rushed to him. His two sisters cried tears of relief when they saw him safe but his mother was stoically poised. She held his hand, pulled him to the side, and said, "Thank God, you came home in one piece. I am not sure what is going on but we aren't going to be safe here, it sounds."

"What are we going to do?" asked Hassan.

"I am not sure about that either, but we need to stay together. Do you hear me?"

"Yes, Hooyo."

"You are the oldest and the only man in this house. I want you to know that your sisters need you more than ever."

"I know, Hooyo, I know."

Still holding on to his hand, the mother turned to her girls and motioned them to a group-hug. Then she lifted her head, led them into the house, and locked the door behind them.

A throng of Somali refugees had walked hundreds of miles to reach sanctuary in camps just across the Kenyan border. Within it, one particular mother with two adolescent daughters drew the attention of the western humanitarians rushing about in frantic attempts to bring order and supplies to the camps. The mother was crying inconsolably and refusing food, medical treatment, and even water, despite her obvious de-hydration. Sounds that would have been hard to comprehend in any language fell constantly from her mouth.

After 20 years of a dictatorial regime's oppression, the capital city of Somalia, Mogadishu, had exploded into a bloody civil war, spitting mobs of violence onto the streets and onto its citizens. Hassan's family and neighbors found themselves fleeing the remnants of an army loyal to a dictator who was about to fall and the armed rebel fighters trying to oust him. Moving in concert, the refugees formed an ant-like line stretching deep into the horizon. Every possible means of transportation was used though the majority trusted nothing but their feet to carry them to safety. Those who had cheated death now could not avert the hunger and exhaustion that was claiming them, as nights became indistinguishable from days. All the while rain poured down on them.

As the day drew to a close, a disoriented Hassan veered with exhaustion from the rest of the group and collapsed in sleep. Alas, he awoke in the middle of the night—alone, scared, and starving. As he tried to find his way back, he accidentally walked east, away from his fleeing countrymen, ever increasing the distance between them.

Unbeknownst to him, the group had camped for the night on the other side of the hilltop just above the tree line of the jungle that was hindering his hearing and view. In urgent haste, Hassan tried to make sense out of this aimless world that seemed devoid of human decency. He could only hear the alien chants of unknown crickets, and howling coyotes in the distance, but not a single human hum. As he scanned the dense darkness, he could not make out a single mark of civilization, not even a flickering light, a throttling engine, or even a neighing mare.

With no sense of direction, Hassan moved on, increasing the miles between himself and the herd. Realizing that he was nowhere near to humankind, he fell into despair. He yearned to cry out, yet was fearful of attracting predators. Wearily, he leaned back onto the trunk of a fig tree for both heat and support, falling asleep again. The next morning, he awoke, cold and shivering, to find that he was still alone in the middle of a jungle. All he could do was weep. And although Hassan seemed to be appropriately dressed for the lackluster East African weather (jeans, turtle neck shirt, tennis shoes and garment to pull over himself), it had not been enough to provide warmth and comfort during the night.

When there were no more tears to be shed, Hassan sat under the tree and watched the tropical leaves dangle lazily while he waited for the worst. The bush was so thick that he couldn't see farther than a few yards. If a leopard, lion, or any other predator made a move on him, Hassan would have been pounced on like a wounded buffalo, with neither the space nor the time to dodge.

Tired of feeling sorry for himself, Hassan decided to try his feet. He walked aimlessly for hours and hours. Eventually, the forest thinned out a little, and he discovered an unused overgrown footpath. Who could guess when the last human feet had set themselves down on this unknown land in the middle of this torrential rain forest? There was no way to tell of course, especially now with the rain.

If there's no trace of other humans for the naked eye to see, Hassan thought fearfully, *there probably aren't other human scents for predators to choose from, aside from my own.*

Throwing caution to the wind, Hassan shouted: "God, please help me out here! You said you would deliver your children from harm's way wherever they were, and that you would hear them whenever they are in need. So OK, God, I'm gonna give you five minutes—no, thirty. No, no, I will give you, oh, I don't know, God. But if you don't give me a sign that you are at least watching, I'm doomed."

Hassan maintained his pace but his stomach growled with a gnawing hunger. For a long while, various chants of different birds were the only sounds of solace. But then in a split second, there it was: the deadliest creature of all. The king of the jungle, the "God of death," was prowling toward him on the same path.

Hassan froze as his eyes locked with the lion's. Neither dodging nor charging, the lion himself stood as though he too was baffled, it seemed, just a leap or two away. Hassan was terrified to see those powerful jaws, the piercing eyes, and the spear-like whiskers. How long would it be, he wondered, before he was going to be a lifeless slab of lunch for this lion?

It seemed an eternity before the lion turned on his side, emitted a soft growl, and marked the ground three and three: three with his left hind leg and three with his right. He then sat back on his hindquarters as though he were provoking Hassan to unravel the inscrutable puzzle.

Confused, Hassan remained motionless as he searched his mind for a suitable reply. Suddenly, he recalled a legend told by his uncle about how lions could entertain an oath with men: if a lion marks three and three parallel lines with his hind legs on the ground, one has to follow suit by doing the same. So in order to simulate the ritual, a human being has to lower himself to the ground on all fours and respond in kind. The legend says that the purpose of this significant ritual was to communicate to men that the lion was entering an oath of intent to harm no one. He would, in fact, protect human beings who enter an oath with him as he would his own cubs. In return, the lion would expect the person on oath to maintain a contract of secrecy. The person must never reveal the whereabouts of any lion, even if or when it kills livestock. If the pledge is breached, the lion is obligated to abandon it all for revenge.

If the legend were true, it was now or never. So Hassan followed the same steps, repeating the lion's ritual, grasping at the hope that the lion would let him live another day.

Hassan took a few steps to the side, giving the lion a little more room to pass but placing himself behind a huge canopy's truck on the edge the footpath just in case. The lion took the offer, passed him by, then stopped in a few yards, turned around, started walking, stopped, turned around, started walking, repeating the ritual long enough for Hassan to guess that he was signaling for him to follow. When Hassan still didn't make a move, the lion sat back on his hind parts and softly roared.

In disbelief that he was still in one piece, Hassan began to think that the lion was not considering him as his next meal, yet he could not help but wonder whether the oath had any bearing. And if it did, how binding and how long was it going to last?

"Well," Hassan said to himself, "I shall have to wait and see."

Again, the lion stood up, looked away as though he were ready to resume a journey, but then noticed that Hassan was still not following. He grunted softly and sat back. Hassan stood still. The lion repeated the ritual four times more. Finally, the lion moved westward, as he possibly had come to the conclusion that he had offered Hassan enough opportunity.

Hassan looked on as the lion disappeared into the forest. He listened but soon the gentle crunch beneath the lion's bare feet faded into the distance. Lingering silence seemed to follow when suddenly, the chirping and twittering of a great number of birds seethed through the air with disquieting calls. Was it a warning to tell all that the king of danger had arrived? Or was it simply a fair greeting from his fellow habitat-mates? Hassan could not tell. All he knew was that the tumult increased to a decibel level that disturbed his mind. And when he thought it could not get worse, the world around him awoke with even more wails. Baboons began to yowl, chipmunks and squirrels bluffed with alarming "eeks," and countless other cries he could not name …... Trepidation took hold of him. What was the lion up to? Was he coming back to waste him now? But where? Was the lion behind him, waiting to pounce? Did he go just to gather friends, planning to beat him dead? Hassan was a mess.

Looking around and about, he spotted a baobab tree and, not fully aware of his intent, he clambered close to the top. At 20 feet, Hassan found a sizeable seat where the boughs departed the trunk. Relieved that he was safe, he rested there. Minutes passed before calm returned all at once. The chaotic choir ceased with an uncertain hush punctuated by the branches' involuntary sway, and an occasional flirting pair of birds that fluttered by. Hassan balanced his body against the base of the boughs.

He mulled over his reality but solutions refused to emerge from his agony. The day proceeded and hunger began to harass him. Time was moving ever so slightly yet shadows thickened, followed by dissonant songs that the forest inhabitants saw fit to sing.

The day moved slowly. Hassan was fully cognizant that when nighttime arrived, it would not come with bouquet and banquet to please him.

Suddenly, the lion emerged from the entangled bush with a no-sound-to-disturb-a-soul saunter. Not a note of the earlier alarms were set off this time. He approached the tree Hassan was in, lifted his gaze, looked up, grunted three times, turned lazily, and walked away. In a few steps he slowed down, stopped, grunted three times again, then sat down.

Hassan, talking to himself, said, "I have no idea what this lion is up to but if I want to survive, I have to trust the oath. Besides, he has to eat sometime. So he is eventually going to lead me to where he can find a meal, which means, perhaps, that there are domesticated animals and human beings somewhere nearby. I have to follow him."

He dismounted from the tree, took three steps towards the lion, stopped and looked.

The lion stood up and grunted three times.

Hassan walked towards him tentatively. As he took a few more steps, the lion proceeded on his way. A few feet back, Hassan paced after him. Soon he began to feel a bit more secure about his company. As they went on, the lion intermittently stopped to rest in the shade of the trees. Soon Hassan thought that he was enjoying the leisure as much as the lion.

He relaxed as he sensed that the lion himself was collected and calm. In fact, he thought the two had built a bit of an invisible bond.

Finally, although they were still in the forest, they felt a warm, helpful wind on their faces. At that moment, the lion made an abrupt turn towards a tree. Wondering what had caused the sudden change in direction, Hassan followed. As they got closer, Hassan could make out ripe berries festooned on the branches, a bounty of berries lying on the ground. The lion yawned, took his position in the shadow of the tree and, shaking his mane at Hassan, signaled to him. Hassan understood this to mean, "Come on, Hassan. It's all yours!"

Hassan squatted cautiously, keeping an eye on the lion. He picked a berry and felt its sweetness burst ecstatically in his mouth. Frantic, he began to gather as many berries as his hands could hold. The lion unfolded his forelegs and laid his head down on them as though he were saying, "Take your time, kid, please. We are in no hurry."

Despite his apprehension, Hassan grabbed the fallen fruits and threw them down his gullet. Then, while the lion watched, Hassan climbed up into the tree and began grazing on one bundle of berries after the other.

At last he was satisfied, and not only had his hunger dissipated but miraculously his anxiety had vanished as well and his loneliness abated. He forgot his predicament. He came down from the tree at peace with himself, faced the lion, and started chattering.

"Oh my God, I'm not dead! And I'm not starving anymore! I could just kiss you!"

The lion hitched his head a little, his yellow-green eyes darting about.

"Hey," Hassan said in a worried voice, "I hope I didn't offend you. But you should know that you are the first lion friend that I have had. Well, so far you seem to be a friend, and I hope you will not change. Oops, please allow me to correct myself. You are the first friend from the animal kingdom that I have ever had, period. And listen, I would have you know that it was not my fault at all. Not having a friend wasn't my fault, I mean, you understand?"

He realized that the lion was paying no attention to him whatsoever.

The lion turned his head a little to the right, then to the left, gazing off into the jungle.

"What?" said Hassan. "Are you saying that my lack of friendship and familiarity with your tribe is discriminatory? Hey, be fair, because I was going to say that myself, OK. I am ashamed that I've never had a lion friend before, too. Yet again, you must understand that we human beings think that you are a threat to us. All members of the cat family are. To be honest, I really didn't think but…?"

Now the lion raised his head and laid it back on his shoulder.

"You think I am lying, don't you?" said Hassan. He babbled on: "Well, you got me. I am lying through my teeth. Yes, yes, I thought so too. I was really scared of you. I thought that you were a threat to all mankind and to me. You would not blame me for that, would you? Well, what you should know is that I have never met anyone like you, since I have spent all my time with those ferocious machine-gun toting Homo sapiens. Had I known what I know now, I swear to you, I would have been a totally different person. By the way, you must sincerely believe me when I swear. You know that in my religion, and speaking of religion, what is your take on that? Well, please don't answer that. Anyway, what I was trying to say was that, in my religion, one never swears to God in vain."

The lion lifted his head and jerked his ears back and forth.

"What? You don't believe me, do you?"

The lion grunted, and shook his mane.

"Wow! I just realized that humans are not the only tribe who are bound by an oath. You have also shown your integrity by honoring your oath," Hassan said.

The lion growled, put his head on the ground, and closed his eyes.

"Are you telling me that I talk too much, Mr. Lion?"

The lion sleepily opened his eyes and blinked twice.

"I can't believe you're saying yes to that. Is it really that bad, sir? Well, my own mother told me long ago that I talk too much, but I am sure your mother said that to you, too. My friend, the problem is even if that is true, I can't do anything about it. I just talk and talk!"

The lion straightened his head and pointed both his ears towards Hassan.

"All right, all right. I'll try to improve. But can I at least air my opinion in moderation?"

The lion blinked his eyes once and once more again.

"Wow, was that a yes? And another, all right!" Hassan chanted. "What a deal, what a democratic joy it is to live amongst you guys! Hey, Mr. Lion, let me ask you another question, sir."

Hassan looked at the lion and saw that his eyes were shut. "Are you sleeping? Anyway, I bet that you aren't asleep yet even if you are trying, so I will go on. Are your friends, I mean the rest of the lion kingdom, as nice as you, sir?"

The lion waved his tail, menacing.

"Oh, you are kidding me! They aren't? What the heck! Well, I have you on my side and that is all that matters to me," Hassan boasted. "But, hey, Friend, do you know that you have not told me your name yet?"

The lion raised his head, and again shook it a bit.

"You think having a name is silly, right? Well, I think so too. But that is what people do where I am from, giving everything a name, OK. So my friend, in sickness and health, let us unite for the sake of names. Since I already have one, let me tell you that mine is Hassan. From now on yours will be Kamal. By the way, in case you are wondering, Kamal means 'complete' or 'sufficient' in Arabic. I am not sure whether it matters much to you but I am a Somali. My native tongue is Somali too. Very strange, right? My point is, I would have preferred to call you a Somali name, yet right as we speak I don't feel like it. Well, honestly, I cannot think of one in Somali now. So let us have Kamal as your rightful name, OK?"

"Now, Kamal, I am really thirsty. I guess what I am asking is if you, by any chance, happen to know any place around here where we can get a drink. And please keep in mind that we are both tired. Frankly, if you aren't, I am. So let's not walk too far, OK?"

It seemed that Kamal had been following everything Hassan had been saying all along, because he abruptly stood up, stretched his legs, and began to move on.

"Wow, you are serious, Kamal, aren't you?" chattered Hassan. "Well, I can tell that you are ready to carry on, but frankly, I'm a little apprehensive about leaving all this fruit behind. Can we at least take some with us? You may not care much for it but I do."

The lion kept on moving.

"Oh. Just like that, Kamal, hah? You are going to move on without me, right? You aren't going to wait for me? OK, fine then. I am going to climb back up and collect some fruit in my robe and I will catch up with you in no time, you will see."

Hassan darted back to the tree, scaled it, and using his over-all-garment as a bucket, gathered the half-ripened berries. While he was in the tree, he kept his eyes on Kamal, who seemed to be patiently waiting a few feet away.

Hassan gingerly climbed down with his loot and walked over to Kamal, eventually coming closer to him than ever before. Kamal rose to his feet, gave a wide yawn, and, nonchalant, moved south, pausing every so often to sniff the air and survey the pathway.

About an hour before sunset, Kamal stopped, perked up his ears, and broke into a trot. Hassan was a bit disturbed by this behavior. He did not know whether Kamal was going to leave him now for a fight with an unknown enemy or was about to catch a meal.

He hesitated and slowed his pace, trying to stay out of the way of whatever danger was about to unfold.

Kamal crouched and scrunched his head down into his mane. Hassan also crouched down and crept closer and closer to Kamal. It was then that he spied what Kamal appeared to be stalking! And it was not a meal but a well, brimming with sparkling, spring water. In earnest, Hassan began to drink from the far end, opposite Kamal.

By now Hassan was purely baffled with Kamal's ability to

understand him, as well as Kamal's generosity. He sat on the edge of the well, staring at Kamal.

"Kamal," he finally uttered, "I am absolutely stunned. You are a genius, sir!"

Kamal yawned.

"Oh, how dumb I am! You already know that, too, hah?"

The lion raised his head and began to lick himself. As the urgency of cleansing himself continued, Hassan stood up and walked towards his preoccupied friend.

"Kamal," he said, "it occurred to me that sunset is approaching, and I am guessing that this place isn't an ideal spot to settle in for the night. I would suggest that you and I…" he pointed his finger at Kamal and then to himself, "search for a more hospitable place. You probably don't care where you spend the night, but I do. After all, we all know that you are the 'king of the jungle' and no one in his right mind would dare to bother you, though I have to admit there are too many fools in this universe. But you should keep in mind that you are no longer alone. You have this fragile life to take care of as well."

Kamal did not respond. Hassan ate his berries and then stopped, deciding that it was better to save some for later.

Kamal sniffed about as though he were ready to move on.

Hassan said, "Kamal, I am not ready yet, OK."

Kamal lowered himself to the ground, rolled onto his back, wallowed in the dampened earth, then quickly got to his feet and took off.

"Hey, hey," Hassan cried. "You are a bit stubborn, wouldn't you say so yourself, sir?"

Kamal bellowed once, and followed with another, stronger roar, then another and another in a faster and more furious tone, then letting out four to five softer hiccups.

"Kamal, take it easy, Friend. I was just kidding. Man, aw man, I didn't know that you are that sensitive!"

Within minutes, Kamal came to a halt next to a thick fig tree that would provide warmth by blocking the wind and also would defend them against unwarranted attacks from behind.

Inexplicably, Kamal did not claim the best position for himself but, like a devoted father, stepped back and took a seat 30 feet away.

Hassan did not hesitate to take advantage of this opportunity, and claimed ownership to the most preferable spot under the tree. "Thanks, Kamal. Very generous of you," he chattered, trying to make himself as comfortable as he could. "Nice bed," he went on, as he felt about, trying to decide where to lie down. "Did you make this bed yourself? Well, you don't have to answer that question."

Hassan started collecting leaves and branches, twisting them off the nearby trees. He placed them on the ground under the tree, pluming a bed and pillow for himself. He curled into a comfortable ball.

"Hey, Kamal," said Hassan, "I'd share this bed with you, but you didn't ask. I don't understand it, my friend! Do you have a problem with asking?"

The lion grunted.

"Well, if you don't have a problem, I guess I'll see you tomorrow. Sweet dreams, my friend."

Then he had another thought. "Oh, I almost forget to ask you, Kamal, you aren't going to leave me alone tonight in this godforsaken place, are you? If you do, I have to tell you and maybe the world around, that it would be the darkest betrayal in a decade. You don't want to make a black mark on your otherwise impeccable record, do you?"

Though there was no response from the lion, Hassan's

tone and spirit remained high. "Hey, Friend, would you like some of my berries?"

Kamal gave no response.

"Well, if you don't say anything, I'll take that as a no. Believe me, I understand that a few berries would not fill up that belly of yours—but they're better than nothing, right? You haven't had a bite since we met, you know. Anyway," he rattled on, "it's getting too dark to read your sign language. So how about see you tomorrow!"

Though Hassan felt somewhat at ease and connected to this majestic animal, the most feared of the animal kingdom, he was still unsettled. What would Kamal be up to during the night? It occurred to him that it was not exactly fear that was making him uneasy, but the uncertainty of what was going to happen next. Soon, however, his exhaustion won over his anxiety. His eyelids began to droop as he let out a yawn and curled into a tighter ball. He lapsed into a trance and, in a few minutes, he was snoring loudly.

In the middle of the night, Hassan woke up to the sensation of a heavy warm comfort over his entire body. He opened his eyes and couldn't believe what he saw. Kamal had come over to him, and was nestled snuggly against him. Hassan was so grateful. He felt compelled to reciprocate this unconventional act of love from an animal stamped the "Enemy of Men." He freed his hands and began to rub Kamal's belly, neck, and jaws. In return, Kamal stretched and rolled over, feasting on the pleasure of human touch.

The next morning when Hassan awoke, Kamal was again calmly situated 30 feet away. Hassan wanted to hug him, thanking him for his warmth during the night. Yet he was still cautious in his approach as he slowly bent over Kamal and gently rubbed his tail, then his rump and back.

With gratification, Kamal rolled over and, with his hind legs up, folded the front paws on his chest.

"Kamal, you're a classy guy. You like a massage, don't you? Do you want some more?" Hassan rubbed Kamal's belly. In seconds, Kamal began to stroke Hassan with his gentle paws. What had happened to the sharp, powerful claws, the crushing jaws, and the insatiable hunger for fresh flesh? He marveled that this unselfish noble companion lay beneath the myth of a treacherous, murderous beast. He wanted to shout to the whole world how tenderhearted Kamal was, that even a lion could give and receive love!

Hassan watched and followed behind as Kamal roamed and explored the jungle around them. By now Hassan had caught on to some of Kamal's behavior. If Kamal stopped and raised his head, lifting his nose into the air and jerking his ears forward, he was on to something.

Suddenly Kamal crouched down on all four limbs, raising one paw, and then freezing his pose before taking the next step.

Hassan was also frozen as his eyes spied Kamal's prey. Out of nowhere a herd of wildebeest were heading their way. Hassan hunkered to the ground and was still, trying not to spook off the impending kill.

Kamal, too, suddenly changed his tactical maneuver and lay low, lurking in a cover of lush, green grass. The herd advanced, unaware of the impending calamity. When the herd was within 35 feet, Kamal sprang, exploding like a nightmare and, with mighty speed, landed on a male wildebeest.

The kill looked swift with immediate asphyxiation. However, as Hassan drew close, he noticed the faint beat of a pulse. Kamal raised his head, closed his ferocious jaws, and looked at Hassan as though he were inviting him to feed himself first.

What an aberration in nature, for only a mother cheetah would abstain from eating her kill before her cubs had had their fill.

"You never cease to amaze me," Hassan cried. "You want to share the kill with me? I really, really appreciate that you are giving me the honor of making the final kill. But, I have no weapon. I have no knife and I have no fire for cooking. Most importantly, I am queasy about taking a life. I promise though, that the next time I will be ready. Otherwise I will not last a week here."

Kamal sat, raised his head, and roared softly as though he were gurgling water deep in his gullet.

"Oh, come on, Kamal," said Hassan, "I know, I know. I know it's not the time nor the…"

Before Hassan finished his speech, Kamal came over and began feasting on his prey, now totally lifeless, as though he were saying to Hassan, *To heck with your arrogant Homo sapiens self*. In a minute, his munching on a mouthful of lean meat reminded Hassan of his berries hoarded last night. He untied his robe and ate his lunch alongside Kamal.

In the afternoon, Kamal and Hassan went back to the well for another drink of cool water. But Hassan was still preoccupied with how to share the next meal with Kamal. Slowly, he remembered his uncle's tales—the tales of lions and their mythical world. As he sat, he began to remember more of the tales and the lessons for survival that were intertwined in those tales. Through story-telling, his uncle had taught him how to make fire using sticks and dried grasses, how to make knives from stone, and how to get water from roots.

Piecing together the lessons and the tales while staring at a patch of green grass and a fat piece of wood, Hassan cried out with joy. He picked up the piece of wood and scratched a hole in the middle with a sharp stick. He gathered nearby dried and semi-dried grasses, placing them in the center of the hole. Then gouging and concaving into the log's hole with his sharpened stick, he labored until both the stick and the log became hot and a smoking ember sparked onto the dried grass. He gently blew on the ember and then, lo and behold—

FIRE!

Having now solved the problem of creating fire, Hassan decided to abandon the other puzzle of what to do about a knife for another day. Night fell and a pattern began to emerge of Hassan falling asleep a safe distance away from Kamal and then awakening during the night to the lion's warm, soft body snuggled against him.

Starting at the crack of dawn the next morning, Hassan embarked upon one experiment after another, trying to make a knife that would increase his odds of surviving on the savanna. By midday he had almost perfected his art of stone sharpening by splitting apart countless numbers of stones and then whetting them by rubbing the pieces against a larger stone. Before he knew it, he had made a dozen sharp spear-tipped-like stones for knives.

Within the week, he had figured out how to make bows and arrows with breathless ease. Over the days and weeks that followed, Hassan molded himself into a formidable, skillful hunter of birds, rabbits and, sometimes, even deer. Yet whenever he tried to share his kills with Kamal, the lion friend would politely turn him down by walking away. Hassan interpreted this to mean that Kamal was not going to stoop so low as to scrounge Hassan's petty supply of food.

Life went on. The routine of hunting then seeking water

and a warm place to park became a ritual and Hassan settled into a cave man's life, accepting the lion as his friend, parent, and protector. Then one day, as they were taking their usual prowl through the dense jungle and neighboring savanna, Kamal suddenly changed his prowling pattern, stopping frequently to sniff the ground and surrounding flora.

Closely watching Kamal, Hassan remembered a substitute teacher, a conservationist (which itself was an oddity in Somalia) from his early school years. The teacher had taught the class about the mating rituals and territorial habits of the jungle denizens. Lions, he remembered learning, mark their territory and leave mystical messages of matrimonial eligibility throughout the wilderness.

This must be what Kamal is doing, thought Hassan. *Kamal is advertising for a suitable mate.*

What Hassan did not figure out, however, was that Kamal was already on the trail of a female lion who had left disguised messages about her own love for the most eligible, bachelor lion.

"Yes, Kamal," Hassan chuckled, "I have been thinking about it too, Friend: leaving love messages to lure a mate! Yes, it is about time we have some female companionship around here. We are both in need of some kind of....change, don't you think? By the way, don't count me out. You never know, I may find a wild female who has chosen to live in this free-from-it-all world, just like me." He saw the lion looking at him.

"Well, you are right. Mine wasn't the textbook example of one who chose to leave. It wasn't exactly my own decision but now I am having a blast…!"

Before Hassan finished his sentence, Kamal had already set off, scampering in a way that was new to him.

"Hey, where the hell are you going?" shouted Hassan.

But Kamal was by now too engaged to heed his plea. Far

ahead, a solo, tawny lioness came strolling into view out of the brush.

Kamal slowed but continued to approach with a spirited saunter. Then he sat down on his hindquarters and growled. As the lioness came closer, they both roared at each other. Kamal made the first move with very subtle but seductive signs of saluting her—tail up, mane roused, with eyes fixed strictly on her. The lioness remained wary of such behavior and so revealed a tenacity that a lioness usually deploys when she is about to slap. Crouching, she bared it all, canines and claws, and roared with rage. Kamal was forced to withdraw. He pulled his tail down, lowered his head and neck, turned aside, moved a few feet away and sat with eyes averted.

Hassan moved close enough to witness the ceremonial courtship.

"That's a hell of a beautiful lady, Kamal," Hassan cried from a distance.

Kamal stood up but looked nervous. He turned his head to Hassan.

"Aw, maaaan, you can't be serious. Are you asking me what to do next?"

Kamal cocked his head, and then sank back down to the ground.

"Oh, come on. It isn't that hard, Kamal. Is she playing hard to get? Are you going to let her get away with that?"

The lion perked up his ears, stood up, and began to walk slowly towards the lioness.

"There you go. I knew you could follow a friend's advice," barked Hassan.

The lioness roared, bared her killer canines, perked back her ears, and crouched on all fours, again feinting to lunge. Kamal startled, jumped back a few feet, raised his tail, waved it, looked at her, then looked at Hassan. Hassan started laughing hysterically.

The situation seemed ominous. Every time Kamal approached the lioness, she would lunge at him, claws and canines bared. She showed no interest in courtship. Worse, it looked as though she were going to draw blood if she were not left alone. Minutes went by. Then hours. Yet the two parties remained at a stalemate.

As the day grew old, Hassan lost all curiosity and fell asleep.

Late in the afternoon, Hassan awoke to the sights and sounds of festive feline lovemaking off in the distance. The couple seemed to copulate every five minutes or so. At times the lioness would lure the lion by standing up, licking her lips (fork-like whiskers and all), rubbing herself on him, then turning away, enticing him with her voluptuous hind quarters. When he did not leap on her with lust, she would offer a most endearing allure, which no male in the universe would have been able to refuse, and submissively laid herself right down before him, pure and simple.

It did not take long for Hassan to change his mind. "Kamal and Whatever-her-name-is!" he cried. "You guys should be ashamed of yourselves. Having sex right before my eyes? Whatever happened to 'Thou shall not sin'? Because, let's face it, you have had no matrimonial ceremony that I am aware of. By the way, do I have to remind you that I am barely of age?"

Hassan's words apparently had no effect for he realized that no sooner had he said them than they were at again.

"Oh, oh," Hassan snorted. "Now you think that I am jealous of you and you're rubbing it in, hah?"

Kamal roared and jerked up his ears.

"That's ridiculous, Kamal. It really is. And if you're thinking that I wish I had a girlfriend, you must be insane, my friend. No, no, no, not me."

Kamal stood up, hesitated, and sat back again, growling.

Hassan's eyes glazed over as his mind briefly drifted off. "Well," he went on, "frankly, I wouldn't mind knowing someone with that kind of infatuation for me!"

Kamal ignored him and he and his mate were at it again.

"That's it," Hassan said. "I can't take this anymore."

He rose to his feet and began walking toward the two enthralled lovers, completely unaware of the danger of encroaching upon this highly charged space.

Kamal watched him, wary, and, realizing that Hassan was heading their way, patted his girlfriend on her shoulder with his paw. She rose to her feet and stretched. Kamal turned and looked directly at Hassan; he let out a roar before slinking off into the brush with the lioness by his side.

What's happening? Where are they going? wondered Hassan. It was then that he realized that he had crossed the line. The lioness had not been a party to the oath between Kamal and Hassan. She would have seen him as an enemy, a threat, and she could have attacked, tearing him into shreds.

"Hey," Hassan shouted, his heart pounding. "I didn't mean it."

He sat down, closed his eyes, and took a few deep breaths. It took him a few seconds to fully realize how close he had come to death. Once again Kamal had honored their oath and changed the course of Hassan's fate.

He looked around at the lengthening shadows and noticed that the sun was low on the horizon. Soon darkness would ensue. For the first time in months, he felt lonely and uncertain about what lay ahead and what the night might bring. Danger lurked behind every shadow. Quickly, he scrambled to the top of a nearby acacia tree to take refuge for the night. It was far from the comfort that he had become accustomed to—cozying up with Kamal—but it provided the bare minimum necessary for survival.

With the early morning sun creeping into the sky, Hassan awoke. Looking down at the ground beneath him, he spotted Kamal leaning against the trunk of the tree. He scanned the surrounding area warily, hunting for the lioness. But Kamal was alone. His sizzling love companion was no longer with him.

Hassan rapidly descended, sat next to Kamal, rubbed his neck, hugged him, and said, "Hey, Kamal, what happened to your girlfriend? Let me guess, it was one of those one night stands, right?"

Kamal stretched his neck, tilted it a bit and yawned.

"Oh, come on, are you saying yes? Come on. Give me a break. I bet she threw you out. Admit it, man. I suppose you spent the night prowling the jungle, bad mouthing her to your friends. Oh God, guys everywhere, of all species, are the same!"

Kamal rolled over on his side, laid his head on the ground, and closed his eyes.

"Yeah, it's better to admit it. Yeah, take your whipping like a man. Lick your wounds and move on. But can I tell you what's funny about it all?"

The lion flicked an ear up.

"You're going to think I'm crazy, but I don't feel sorry for you at all. I don't regret that you lost her, because now I've gained you back."

The lion growled.

"Are you asking me why? Are you out of your mind, Friend? Simple, first of all, I have to admit to you that I was jealous of you. And second, she was no friend of mine. Who knows what

she was going do next, once she had her way with you, eat
both of us alive or what?"

Kamal collected himself and began grooming, as though he
were cleansing himself of Hassan's embarrassing admission.

"Yeah, yeah. It's true," Hassan said.

Hassan had but barely finished his statement when Kamal
stood up and let out a stream of thunderous bellows. His gut
belched, his mouth drooled, and his eyes watered. Hassan
tried to calm him down but to no avail. He wondered if his
lion friend was falling sick from the intense, uninterrupted,
shameful sharing. Then Kamal abruptly stood up and ambled
away, toward the south.

Hassan, who was in no position to guess what was on
Kamal's mind, followed. It did not take him long, however, to
realize that Kamal had a long journey in mind.

They walked all day and through the night, passing through
open land with scattered trees, then valley-beds. Then, on
the third day, they came across a land fattened with thick, tall
trees. As a maroon sunset sent its dying rays across the
horizon, they reached the edge of a plateau on which a cluster
of camps stood, huddled together.

Kamal, still leading the way, bore to the left as though
he were singling out a particular victim in a herd. This time,
however, there was no herd, just sets of thatched enclosures
with tents and huts hugging each other. Detached from this
community was another set of thatched enclosures, situated
as though to guard the rest. Perhaps a half-mile away from
the camp, Kamal finally stopped. He sat back on his hind legs
and emitted a long yawn. When Hassan caught up with him,
he crouched next to Kamal, trying to rub his chest. But Kamal
hastily stood up on all fours and, as though in a hurry, grunted,

stretched his forelegs, pulled out his claws, and marked three lines in succession on the ground!

Hassan watched intensely and realized that this was the end of his relationship with Kamal. Kamal had kept his oath— nurtured, nursed, and protected Hassan and now had brought him back to a semi-civilization. Tears falling, Hassan looked at his friend.

"This is it, hah?" he sobbed.

Kamal looked away.

"Well, you know Kamal, I am going to mi..."

Kamal interrupted him with a growl.

"OK, OK, I can't keep you with me any longer. Your enemy is all around us today," Hassan said, wiping tears away from his face. He bent down, picked a pebble from the ground, marked three parallel lines, just like the lion, and said, "There you have it, King. There you have it."

Kamal faced Hassan, lifted a paw, and delicately tapped on his thigh. He then turned and regally walked away, as though they had never met.

Hassan stood there in awe and for the first time in years did not follow Kamal. He watched the lion depart, strolling away with an unmatched grace that no one could imitate, until he disappeared down the hillside, behind the brush, beyond Hassan's limited sight.

After what seemed an eternity, Hassan took a few tentative steps toward the unknown world, eyeing the closest tent. Who were these people and would they be able to help him locate his family, his clan?

Cautiously approaching, and through tear-filled eyes, he watched a young girl come out of the tent, pick up a rake, and begin cleaning the yard. She resembled a memory of long ago—the memory of a little girl in his life. As he drew closer, his eyes began to clear and then he froze. This was his young sister who was raking the yard—Iftin, older now and all grown.

The girl looked up from her raking and spied the wild-looking man with a long, straggly beard, wearing a rabbit skin around his waist. She took one terrified look at him, screamed, and ran off.

Hassan shouted after her, calling her name, imploring her to wait and trying to assure her that all was well. He was only her brother who had been lost. By the time she came to her senses, it was too late for her to be honored with a long awaited, blessing hug. Both her older sister and their mother had heard Hassan's wailing, recognized his voice and, push-ing past her, rushed out of the tent in the midst of shrills of shocked joy. In minutes, all the neighbors heard the howls of happiness and were out on the scene. In less than an hour, the whole camp, old and young, were at the family's tent.

"It has been three years, it has been three..." his mother repeated endlessly, tears streaming from her eyes. But now the tears that had been shed in sadness were tears of joy. And these were tears that she did not mind sharing.

"Three years, three years," Hassan's mother murmured in disbelief. "Three years, three years, it has been three years."

ACKNOWLEDGEMENTS

No matter the size or page numbers, a book is a collective work. Thus, I would like to express my gratitude to Maggi Larson, Margaret Beegle, Ahmed I. Samatar, Lidwien Kapteijns, and Becky Powers.

My utmost appreciation goes to Jessica Powers whose tireless effort brought this book into being.

Lastly, thanks to my lovely wife Suad Ateyah and my son Sahan (Saleh) Yusuf.

OTHER BOOKS FROM CATALYST PRESS

Dark Traces, *by Martin Steyn*

The body of a teenage girl is found in the veld near an upper middle-class suburb of Cape Town, South Africa. The pathologist remembers a similar case. The last thing recently widowed Detective Jan Magson feels like taking on is a serial killer file, but alongside Inspector Colin Menck, he follows the trail. And every time a lead reaches a dead end, Magson finds himself looking down at another dead girl, wondering how he's going to make it through the dark traces of yet another night, alone, a service pistol at his side.

Sacrificed, *by Chanette Paul*

Rejected by her parents, sister, husband, everyone except her extraordinary daughter, Caz Colijn lives a secluded life in her own little patch of Africa. But a single phone call from her estranged sister shatters her refuge. From the Congo's sparkling diamond mines to Belgium's finest art galleries, from Africa's civil unrest to its deeply spiritual roots, *Sacrificed* seamlessly crosses borders and decades with a fiercely captivating story.

We Kiss Them With Rain, *by Futhi Ntshingila*

Life wasn't always hard for fourteen-year-old Mvelo. But now her mother is dying of AIDS and what happened to Mvelo remains unspoken, despite its growing presence. *We Kiss Them With Rain* explores both humor and tragedy in this modern-day fairytale set in a squatter camp outside of Durban, South Africa, in which the things that seem to be are only a façade and the things that are revealed and unveiled create a happier, thoroughly believable, alternative.

Love Interrupted, *by Reneilwe Malatji*

In her debut collection of short fiction, Reneilwe Malatji invites us into the intimate lives of South African women, their whispered conversations, their love lives, their triumphs and heartbreaks. This diverse chorus of female voices recounts misadventures with love, family, and community in powerful stories woven together with anger, politics, and wit.

BOOKS BY STORY PRESS AFRICA, an imprint of Catalyst Press

Shaka Rising: A Legend of the Warrior Prince
a graphic novel by Luke Molver

A charismatic young warrior prince emerges from exile to usurp the old order and forge a new, mighty Zulu kingdom. This retelling of the Shaka legend explores the rise to power of a shrewd young prince who must consolidate a new kingdom through warfare, mediation, and political alliances to defend his people against the expanding slave trade.

AUTHOR'S BIO

After fleeing Somalia, **Ahmed Ismail Yusuf** lived in several states but has lived in Minneapolis, Minnesota since 1997. He did not speak English when he arrived, he was a high-school dropout, and he was not sure what his actual age was. Today he has two college degrees and is the author of *Somalis in Minnesota*, published by the Minnesota Historical Society Press, and *Gorgorkii Yimi*, a collection of stories in Somali, published by Ponte Invisible. In February 2018, The History Theatre of St. Paul, Minnesota will produce his play, "A Crack in the Sky," a memoir about how Yusuf found inspiration in Maya Angelou and Malcolm X during his early days as an immigrant to the U.S.